"You're having dirty thoughts. Your hip movements are lewd."

HiGH sCHOOL

DxD

2

THE PHOENIX OF THE SCHOOL BATTLE

Th-that's...

The twins were coming right at me, dragging their chain saws along the floor!

"The flame of the immortal firebird burns within me!"
"I will reduce you to dust!"

THE PHOENIX OF THE SCHOOL BATTLE

2

ICHIEI ISHIBUMI

ILLUSTRATION BY
MIYAMA-ZERO

New York

Volume 2
Ichiei Ishibumi

Translation by Haydn Trowell
Cover art by Miyama-Zero

HIGH SCHOOL DxD Vol. 2 SENTO KOSHA NO PHOENIX
©Ichiei Ishibumi, Miyama-Zero 2008
First published in Japan in 2008 by KADOKAWA CORPORATION, Tokyo.
English translation rights arranged with KADOKAWA CORPORATION, Tokyo, through TUTTLE-MORI AGENCY, INC., Tokyo.

English translation © 2021 by Yen Press, LLC

Yen On
150 West 30th Street, 19th Floor
New York, NY 10001

Visit us at yenpress.com
facebook.com/yenpress
twitter.com/yenpress
yenpress.tumblr.com
instagram.com/yenpress

First Yen On Edition: January 2021

Yen On is an imprint of Yen Press, LLC.
The Yen On name and logo are trademarks of Yen Press, LLC.

The publisher is not responsible for websites (or their content) that are not owned by the publisher.

Library of Congress Cataloging-in-Publication Data
Names: Ishibumi, Ichiei, 1981– author. | Miyama-Zero, illustrator. | Trowell, Haydn, translator.
Title: High school DxD / Ichiei Ishibumi ; illustration by Miyama-Zero ; translation by Haydn Trowell.
Other titles: Haisukūru Dī Dī. English
Description: First Yen On edition. | New York, NY : Yen On, 2020.
Identifiers: LCCN 2020032159 | ISBN 9781975312251 (v. 1 ; trade paperback) |
    ISBN 9781975312275 (v. 2 ; trade paperback)
Subjects: CYAC: Fantasy. | Demonology—Fiction. | Angels—Fiction. | High schools—Fiction. | Schools—Fiction.
Classification: LCC PZ7.1.I836 Hi 2020 | DDC [Fic]—dc23
LC record available at https://lccn.loc.gov/2020032159

ISBNs: 978-1-9753-1227-5 (paperback)
       978-1-9753-1228-2 (ebook)

10 9 8 7 6 5 4 3

LSC-C

Printed in the United States of America

CONTENTS

I wanted to protect her.

It didn't have anything to do with pacts or promises.

She had to remain the grand, majestic person I most longed for. The one who ran a hand through her brilliant crimson hair.

So give me your strength, Red Dragon Emperor!

Life.0

The name's Issei Hyoudou—but everyone just calls me Issei.

I'm a second-year in high school, but I'm not really your average student anymore, sorry to say.

I'm a demon, you see. Seriously, I'm not kidding. After a strange sequence of events, I wound up getting reborn as one.

It's not all that important, though. Just think of me as a devilish high schooler.

Anyway, a strange situation was unfolding before me one day, and I had no idea how to handle it.

I mean, it looked like I was in a chapel, surrounded by familiar faces.

"Damn it! Why is Issei the one getting married?!"

"There has to be a mistake! A conspiracy, even!"

My two best friends, Matsuda with his shaved head and Motohama with his thick glasses, fixed hateful glares on me.

"Issei! I want my first grandchild to be a girl!"

"H-how you've grown! It seems like only yesterday you were just a child, thinking of nothing but satisfying your libido!"

My parents were both crying, but why did they have to say such embarrassing things?!

I was wearing a white tuxedo. It looked almost like we were at a wedding. Hold on, it *was* a wedding scene. As if on cue, familiar marriage music began to play.

Hang on! This is my *wedding?!* I stood there, flummoxed by this sudden, bewildering situation. Who was the bride? Just who was I marrying?

"Issei, stop fidgeting," came a voice by my side that I instantly recognized.

When I turned to look, I saw a beautiful young woman. Her crimson hair reached all the way down to her hips. It was Rias Gremory.

She was a high-class, noble demon and the one who'd resurrected me as a member of her Familia. I was really only her servant, though.

Keeping my eyes on Rias proved difficult. I mean, in her wedding dress, she was positively dazzling! Ugh, the prez sure was one hell of a beauty!

Plus, she was standing right next to me! Which meant...

"Rias! You look stunning!"

"Nooo, Rias! Why did you have to choose someone like him?!"

High-pitched screams echoed out from every corner of the chapel. No one was saying anything nice about me, though...

I—I see, so Rias and I are getting married!

Talk about a surprise. Our relationship seemed to have reached this point without me even realizing it, and now we were about to tie the knot.

I wasn't really sure how we had gotten here, but if I really was about to marry my idol, the prez, I didn't have any problem with that!

"Do you promise to love her, to comfort her, to honor, and to keep her for better or for worse—?"

The old priest was running through the typical wedding vows, but my head was overflowing with other thoughts.

If we were getting married, that meant we would be husband and wife. Husband and wife. That meant family. Family meant children. Children meant making babies. Making babies meant sexual relations.

Sexual relations meant life as a married couple…starting on our wedding night. A wedding night!

Come here, Issei.

In my mind, the prez was already waiting for me naked in bed.

That was what this meant, right?! I mean, if we were husband and wife, it was our duty to start a family, right? Children were a necessary part of a family, and to make children required a certain something. And that "something" was sex.

I was gonna bang the prez!

By the time I had come to that conclusion, my mind was already bursting with excitement, and I couldn't stop the roller coaster of my erotic fantasies.

At last I understood why all my previous attempts at relationships had failed. They'd been in preparation for today—for tonight!

Everything had been leading toward my fateful mission!

That wasn't to say I was unprepared, though. I knew more than enough on that subject. For years, I'd been running simulations in my mind all day, every day!

In other words, I was an ace pilot in the training suite! It was finally time for me to graduate to the real thing!

"You may now kiss the bride."

What?!

Right, right, right. I was getting ahead of myself. The prez and I were going to kiss at the altar!

Rias drew close to my face, her eyes shut.

For a moment, I wondered if this was okay. It had to be, right? Steeling myself, I moved in. Her lips looked so soft. Her lipstick was glistening in the light, sending my head spinning.

Soon they would be mine! Just thinking about it was enough to set my blood on fire!

Huffing and puffing through my nose, I tilted my head forward and brought my face toward hers…

* 　 * 　 *

"Looks like you're enjoying yourself there, kid."

…Huh?!

A mysterious voice had echoed inside my head.

The sound was deep and powerful. It felt unfamiliar, but there was also something that told me I should've recognized it instantly. Whatever it was, it had come from somewhere nearby…

"That's right. I'm beside you."

Who could this mysterious voice belong to?

I glanced around, but the chapel had completely disappeared.

Rias was gone as well, along with everyone else. My parents, my friends, everyone!

I didn't even know where *I* was anymore. My senses were failing; it became difficult just to stay upright.

All sound had vanished. Before me was nothing but pure darkness and absolute silence.

What is this?

Prez! Dad! Mom! Matsuda! Motohama!

Despite my calls for those close to my heart, there was no response. What was happening to me?

Who had that voice belonged to?

"Me."

Argh! No sound came from my body, but my heart leaped in surprise.

Anyone else would've done the same at the sight of a giant monster appearing right before them.

The creature possessed large eyes, as red as blood. Beneath them rested a mouth that stretched all the way to its ears, filled with countless, protruding fangs. A thick horn jutted out from its forehead, and its whole body was covered in crimson scales that resembled roiling magma. Its arms and legs were equally huge and adorned with terrifyingly sharp claws. To top things off, the way its wings spread out to either side of its body just made it look even bigger.

Rising before me, that gigantic monster could be described with only one word...

Dragon.

I might not have been able to speak, but that thing, that Dragon, seemed to pull up the corners of its mouth in amused understanding.

"That's right. You've finally noticed. I've been trying to speak to you all this time, but you're so pathetically weak that my words never reached you. At last, it seems you can perceive me."

Whatever this thing was trying to get across, it wasn't making any sense.

"Perceive"? It had been trying to talk to me? How was I supposed to have known that?!

Was it going to eat me or something?

"Eat you? You? Stop joking around. You hardly look palatable. No, I merely wanted to introduce myself to my partner. I expect we'll be fighting side by side quite a bit from here on out."

"Partner"? *Hold on a second. What's all this about?*

Dragon! I tried to say, though no sound escaped my mouth. *Who exactly are—?*

"You know the answer to that, don't you? Surely, the truth is gnawing at you already. Yes, that's right. I'm exactly what you're thinking. We'll talk again soon, partner."

I glanced at my left arm, only to find it covered in red scales. Razor-sharp talons protruded from my fingertips.

Life.1
I'm Working as a Demon!

I opened my eyes to see the familiar ceiling of my room.

Ah, so it was all a dream.

While it had been one of my best, it had also been one of my worst. The dream had started off so wonderfully. I was getting married to the beautiful Rias. Everything had been going so well until…

My heart was pounding. It would've been strange if it hadn't been, especially after a night like that. My breathing was ragged.

I sat upright and wiped the sweat from my brow. Apparently, I'd been sweating buckets.

Upon realizing that I'd brought my left hand to my forehead, I recalled the last moments of my vision before I'd woken up.

That final scene… That red Dragon… It'd been too unreal, too much like some fantasy game.

Thankfully, there was nothing wrong with my arm, even though it had transformed into that of a monster at the end of the dream. Though it looked normal, I knew perfectly well what was dwelling inside it.

I glanced at my clock.

Four thirty… Still a little early.

Taking a deep breath, I pulled my blankets back over me but then suddenly remembered something important.

Jumping out of bed, I started to get ready.

A crimson-haired beauty wearing a red tracksuit was waiting on the street outside my house. It was Rias Gremory.

She was one year my senior and a veritable idol. She was also the president of the Occult Research Club, a group I'd recently become a part of. Just like me, she was secretly a demon.

She turned her azure eyes my way when she realized I was staring at her.

Hurry up now, she seemed to say, her lips moving in a faint smile.

"I'm on my way!" I changed out of my pajamas and into a jogging suit, then dashed out of the house to begin my morning training.

"Heave-ho, heave-ho!"

"Hey, pick it up! Don't drag your feet or I'll add another ten laps!"

Gasping for breath, I coursed through the residential area in the early morning.

The prez was following after me by bicycle, working to keep me fired up. She was as strict as ever.

It had been around a month now since I'd first been reborn as a demon and a member of Rias Gremory's Familia.

Demons were supposed to be summoned by humans and enter into pacts to grant their wishes in exchange for exacting a cost. That was the kind of work we were involved in, and the prez was no exception.

As her servant, I was working under her each and every day, all the while edging closer and closer to achieving my own goal.

Perhaps you're wondering what that goal is. I think it should be pretty obvious by now.

"I…will…be…a…harem king…!" I panted as I ran.

"Indeed. But to do that, you need to start each day with basic training. We need to build up your strength."

The prez was right. I knew that much.

While I was little more than a newly minted demon myself, if I could prove my worth, there was a chance I'd be awarded a noble title of my own one day. That would enable me to have my own servants, just like the prez. Yep! My plan was to bring countless girls into my service, and then my dream would come true!

To do that, I needed to get stronger, just like Rias had said. Strength was essential in demon society. Simply put, the stronger you were, the more you could achieve.

Climbing the ranks through means like knowledge or diplomacy was possible, but I didn't really have much talent in those areas.

Before I could even think about building a harem, I had to increase my physical abilities. That was why I was training so hard every morning.

Still, the prez was one tough drill sergeant.

"I won't accept any weakness in my servants."

She showed no mercy during my morning training sessions.

Each day started with a twenty-kilometer run, followed by a hundred dashes. That might sound like a lot, but it was only the beginning. From there, I had to tackle other exercises like strength training. Rias subjected me to so many activities that I began to lose track.

Demons were creatures of the night, and our powers were strongest while the sun was down. Knowing this, I'd assumed it would be better to train at night rather than early in the morning, but apparently, that wasn't the case. According to the prez, training in the baleful light of the morning sun would help improve a demon's mental fitness as well.

While my muscles were aching every day, the scary thing was that I was actually getting better.

Lately, it even seemed like I was falling into a bit of a groove. That alone was proof of my progress. My physical education classes at school were getting much easier, too. I was becoming faster at sprinting, and long-distance running wasn't nearly as difficult as it had been.

"Phew..." I came to a stop once I'd reached the goal in the park. My whole body was sweating profusely.

"Good work. Okay then, let's move on to the sprints."

The prez flashed a savage grin.

—o●o—

"The higher your basic stats, the more meaningful your abilities," Rias instructed.

"...Sixty-five..."

After completing my morning marathon and sprint through the park, I moved on to the first item in my strength training regimen, push-ups.

The prez was sitting on my back. Her soft buttocks resting against me felt truly delightful, but with the way my arms were screaming with every push, I didn't have an opportunity to savor the sensation.

Still, what could've been better than the plush feel of her callipygian frame?!

Slap!

"Ah!"

Rias had spanked me... A gasp slipped from my mouth. I wasn't exactly a masochist, but still...

"You're having dirty thoughts. Your hip movements are lewd."

"...Th-that's... Sixty-eight... I—I was just thinking how you're sitting on top of me... Sixty-nine... Like you're riding me... Seventy!"

"So you can talk while doing your push-ups, now, Issei? Guess that means you're getting better. Shall we add another hundred?" Rias joked with a grin.

I prayed that was a joke. I could already feel death approaching.

"Hmm, she should be arriving any minute now..."

"Huh? Who?"

No sooner had I asked the question than a familiar voice said, "Excuse me."

Holding myself upright, I glanced in the direction of that voice.

"Issei, President! Sorry I'm late... Eep!"

The blond-haired girl who'd entered, Asia, tripped and fell to the ground.

*   *   *

"Here's some tea, Issei."

"O-oh, thanks."

I sipped at the tea that Asia had brought in a thermos as I took a quick break. My whole body, from my abs through to my back, was jittering with exhaustion.

"What are you doing here, Asia?" I asked.

The blond beauty's cheeks turned pink. "I heard you were training with the president here each morning... So I wanted to encourage you. All I did was bring you something to drink, though."

Asia was so kindhearted! I was moved!

"Asiaaa! I'm touched! Ah, I never expected the day would come when a cute girl said something like that to me!" I cried out with joy before draining my cup.

Asia, with her long blond hair and pale-green eyes, was a former nun. Meaning that she wasn't connected to the Church anymore. She, too, had been reincarnated as a demonic member of Rias Gremory's Familia, much like I'd been.

A month earlier, she'd gotten caught up in a certain incident and had been killed by a fallen angel. Thanks to the prez, however, Asia had been reborn as a demon and so was now one of us.

Incidentally, the fallen angels were the same sort of wicked angels who appear in the Bible and other holy texts. I guess you could say their distinguishing feature was their black wings.

Angels, fallen or otherwise, were our mortal enemies, and there were lots of ongoing petty skirmishes between them and demons. I had fought one myself just last month, only to realize how truly weak I was. That's what had led to me wanting to get stronger. I wasn't going to let Asia suffer like that ever again.

Our master, Rias, the president of the Occult Research Club, looked to be deep in thought as she sipped her own cup of tea.

"What is it, Prez?" I asked.

Emerging from thought, Rias cleared her throat with a small cough.

"No, it's nothing. But this is good timing. There's something I was hoping to see to today, so how about we all go to Issei's house?"

Huh? What? My house? "Good timing"? And what's with that expression on her face?

"It should be arriving right around now," Rias added.

It was only ten minutes later when I found out the answer to the little mystery.

"…Wh-what's all this?" I asked.

I raised an eyebrow at the sight of the cardboard boxes piled up by the entrance to my home.

The sender's name wasn't even written on them. I couldn't help but be suspicious; they looked like the kind of packages you heard about having bombs in them.

Maybe the prez noticed my dubious expression because she said, "Now then, Issei. Do carry these up to your room."

"Huh? Carry them? I-inside?!"

"That's right. These are Asia's belongings. Be a gentleman and bring them inside now, would you?"

"These are Asia's?!"

I was already shocked to my core, but Rias didn't let up, immediately delivering a death blow. "Indeed. From today, Asia will be living here with you."

A family discussion was the kind of meeting that ranked among the most important conferences and assemblies in the world.

My parents, being the most powerful stakeholders in the house, had the highest decision-making authority. The key to these talks would be the degree of skill to which we teenagers were able to negotiate.

Surprisingly, however, my mom and dad, ostensibly the most influential figures at the assembly, were practically huddling together in fear of the prez's negotiating prowess.

Maybe Rias's eyes were exerting some unseen power over them?

"With that said, Mother, Father, won't you consider allowing Asia Argento to lodge with you on a homestay?" At point-blank range, Rias put forth this completely unreasonable request with poise and grace.

Staring fixedly at Asia, my parents exchanged a few whispers. They were furtively glancing my way, too.

My dad cleared his throat. "Asia...was it?" he asked.

"Yes. Um...Father?" Asia responded nervously.

"'*F-Father...*'? Er... I—I don't know how to put this... But it brings joy to my heart to have two beautiful foreign ladies call me that..."

It looked like my dad was getting emotional. I could appreciate that. Surely, it must have felt good, having the prez and Asia, both of them total knockouts, address him as *"Father."*

Heck, I would've been down on my knees if two beautiful girls started calling me *Big Brother.*

"Dear!" My mom poked my dad with her finger.

With that, he snapped back to his senses. "A-ahem! Unfortunately, with our son living here, our home isn't a good choice for a homestay. He's practically the living embodiment of sexual desire. It pains me to say this, but you might be safer staying somewhere else. With another young lady perhaps? I wouldn't be able to forgive myself if something was to happen to you."

That damn geezer sure didn't hold back. *"The living embodiment of sexual desire"*...?

Still, he had a point. It was probably best for a young woman to live with another girl her age. Even my mom was nodding along in approval, adding things like, "That's right, that's right."

If a beautiful blond girl like Asia was to stay with someone positively overflowing with lustful cravings, there was no telling what might happen. There was even a chance of it becoming an international incident. I bet that was what my parents were thinking.

Seriously, though, I really wasn't going to do anything. It was heartbreaking to know my own mom and dad had so little faith in me.

They were still in the dark about Asia and me being demons, and no one had told them about how a fallen angel had tried to use Asia to advance her own goals, either. I doubt they would've believed me even if I tried to explain it. Besides, it was best to keep them out of demon affairs.

So when we discussed things, we left out certain details and added in plenty of others.

Rias didn't seem the least bit concerned by my parents' refusal, and she continued to speak with a broad smile. "What if Asia was to become your daughter?" she offered.

Wh-what?! Prez... That was awfully suggestive...

"What do you mean?"

"Father. Asia trusts Issei deeply. And I feel the same. Your son is very straightforward, and sometimes he isn't very discreet, but he isn't a fool. Rather, there's a fire inside him, a burning passion that propels him forward and helps him overcome whatever obstacles stand in his way. Both Asia and I are drawn to that part of him. Especially Asia. Isn't that right?"

"Y-yes! Issei saved my life. He's my savior. And he helps me out at school all the time. In class, he..." With a warm, happy smile, Asia began to explain everything I had done for her.

She even told my parents about all these minor things that had happened at school. To be honest, I thought she was giving me a little too much credit. Eventually, it got so embarrassing that I wanted to bolt from the room.

My parents nodded along. "Oh, our Issei did that, did he?" "To think that he could be that helpful to someone." They certainly didn't look dissatisfied with what they were hearing. Well, I suppose any parent would've been happy to hear their child being praised so highly, right?

Cutting through the atmosphere of the conversation like a knife,

Rias offered something extreme. "What if this homestay was to also be a form of bridal training?"

"*Bride?!*" Dad, Mom, and I all cried out in shock.

Where did that come from?!

Asia simply wore a confused expression.

My dad started bawling his eyes out. "...With the way Issei is, I was worried I would never have grandchildren," he said while wiping tears from his face. "I've worried for so long now about whether he would be able to take care of himself on his own..."

I was stunned; where had this come from? Why did my own father have such little faith in my future like that?!

Mom was drying her eyes, too. "I never thought he would find someone to love him. I mean, he's Issei, our useless son. I did my best to try to raise him so that he wouldn't embarrass himself out there in the world, but I'd thought it had all been in vain. If I had a time machine, I would try to warn my younger self. I'd say: *Your son will turn into a good-for-nothing who hides his pornographic DVD collection in his plastic-figurine box at the back of his closet. Be careful how you raise him.*"

Whaaaaat?! My secret DVD collection?! How does she know where I stash it?!

Dad gripped Asia's hand. "Asia! He might not amount to much, but can we entrust him to you?"

Asia didn't seem to realize what he was hinting at, and she responded with a bright smile.

At that, Mother burst into a fit of relieved sobbing. The whole thing looked like some kind of soap opera.

"Rias! Asia Argento is more than welcome here! We'll take good care of her!" my dad ecstatically proclaimed.

Pleased, Rias beamed. "Thank you, Father. And you, Issei. I'll leave Asia in your hands. Asia, you'll be staying with Issei's family from now on, so try not to get into trouble. Watch your manners. And do your best to get along with Issei's parents."

"Is it really all right? I mean…I don't want to be…a b-burden…," Asia stammered.

"If you want to familiarize yourself with Japanese culture and the Japanese way of life, there's no better way than by staying with a family like Issei's," Rias continued. "When I asked you who among our members you would most like to stay with, you didn't hesitate to name Issei, did you?"

Now I understood. Up until this whole debacle, Rias had let Asia borrow one of the vacant rooms in the old school building.

"Y-yes. I did say that, but…"

"It's all right, Asia! You can learn about Japan with us! You can even stay here forever!"

Evidently, my dad was really set on having her as his daughter-in-law.

"See? Even Issei's father wants you to stay," Rias said with a grin.

Asia's confusion finally cleared, and she, too, flashed everyone a warm smile. "I understand, President. I'm not entirely sure what's going on, and I know I'm a little clumsy, but Issei, Mother, Father, please look after me."

Mom and Dad had been completely hoodwinked. As far as they were concerned, all that stuff about Asia becoming my wife had been too good to pass up.

With that, the meeting came to an end, and it was decided that Asia and I would start living under the same roof.

"…Bridal training…," Rias muttered. Her expression looked somehow forlorn.

Something about the look on her face filled me with worry.

The first few days living with Asia came and went pretty quickly.

"Isn't the weather nice, Issei? We're playing softball today in PE, you know. I'm looking forward to it. I've never played it before." Asia chatted excitedly as we made our way to school.

To think that I would be walking with a beautiful young woman by my side every day from now on…

I could feel the curious gazes of my schoolmates boring into me as we approached the gate.

"Why are Argento and Hyoudou walking together…?"

"Impossible… What's he playing at…?"

"He wasn't satisfied with making moves on Rias, so now he's going after Asia, too…?"

Students around us gossiped so loudly, they were approaching frenzied shrieks. I suppose I couldn't blame them, though. They didn't need to know much about me to work out that this should've been an impossible situation.

I, an unpopular, sex-obsessed high schooler, had suddenly started hanging out with some of the school's most popular girls.

Not only that, I was making the commute with our beautiful new blond transfer student, a subject on everyone's lips since the day she'd arrived. From an outsider's perspective, it must've seemed inconceivable.

From what I'd gathered, a lot of guys had already confessed to Asia. They'd probably thought that if I'd done it, they could, too. Asia had rejected them all outright, though.

Unfortunately, that meant some people were starting to hold it against me. Heck, even now, I could feel the hatred in their eyes.

Maybe they had the idea that I was fooling around with one girl after another. It was hardly that simple, but whatever.

Heh. Still, it *was* fun to be regarded that way by my classmates. Even if it was all just a massive misunderstanding, I was starting to feel pretty popular.

Yeah! That's right! Eat your hearts out, folks! This is only the beginning! Ha-ha-ha!

"Did something funny happen?"

"Wha—?!"

Asia looked up at me questioningly. Her face was so close to mine that I found myself blushing. I was still pretty new at this, after all.

"N-no, nothing. By the way, Asia, you haven't had any difficulties, have you? In class, I mean. A-are you getting along with the other girls?"

That was what I was most worried about.

Asia had only just transferred here, and she was a former nun. Her previous way of life had been completely detached from the real world, so it wouldn't have come as a surprise to learn she'd run into a few hang-ups.

I was always there to help out, of course, but the most important thing for Asia was that she had the support of the girls. From what I could tell, she was getting along well with the other members of the Occult Research Club, but I wasn't sure about the situation with her classmates. The idea of her getting bullied seemed unlikely, but I couldn't help but worry.

To date, there'd been nothing I saw that suggested anyone was being mean to her, but there was no telling what went on when I wasn't around.

Without the slightest concern on her face, Asia looked to me with a carefree grin. "Everyone is so kind. They're teaching me all sorts of things to help me get used to life in Japan. I've made lots of friends. I was thinking of inviting them to go shopping, actually."

That was reassuring to hear. It sounded like things were going well. Perhaps there'd been nothing to worry about.

With that, we made our way onto campus and up to our classroom. Now that I was sure no one was mistreating Asia, there was only one other issue…

"Asia! Good morning!"

"Good morning, Asia. You look dazzling today."

No sooner did Asia and I walk through the door to our classroom than Matsuda and Motohama appeared before her.

They were my friends and my negative influences. Their perverted personalities were as famous throughout the school as my own.

"Good morning, Matsuda, Motohama," Asia warmly greeted the two of them.

At this, the pair immediately started getting emotional.

"Ah, this is what it feels like, isn't it, Motohama?"

"It sure is, Matsuda. Having a perfect beauty say good morning to you at the start of the day really makes you feel alive."

As was fairly common, my friends were getting rather worked up over something incredibly minor. I guess I would've done the same until recently, however.

Heh-heh, my newfound confidence and generosity sure had changed me.

Thump!

"Gah!"

I'd been trying to act cool for a moment when Matsuda delivered an unexpected gut punch.

"Wh-what was that for, you bald bonehead?!" I exclaimed. Despite my protestations, Matsuda's face broke into a strange grin, and he delivered a sudden low kick.

Damn, that hurts! What the hell's that idiot doing?

"Ha-ha-ha, Issei, my friend. I've heard the news," he said.

"What news?" I asked.

"That you've been coming to school with Asia here."

"Wh-what's wrong with that?"

"It's strange—that's what's wrong with it. Why do you both keep taking the same route each day?"

Oh-ho. I didn't know where the rumors had started from, but I guess my friends had heard the news.

I licked my lips and curled my mouth in a lecherous smile. "Okay then. Matsuda. Motohama. There's something that separates me from the two of you. An insurmountable barrier. I suppose there's really nothing that can be done about it."

"Wh-what are you gloating about?!"

"Y-yeah, come on, Issei. Just because you're friends with Asia here doesn't mean—"

It was time for the coup de grâce. My grin was one of victory. "Asia and I are living together. Under the same roof. Isn't that right, Asia?"

"Yes. I'm staying with Issei and his family."

"—?!"

My friends fell silent at the sight of Asia's happy smile. It looked like they'd been rendered speechless.

Heh. Ha-ha-ha! Ha-ha-ha-ha-ha-ha-ha! Victory was mine!

"Impossible!" Matsuda blurted out. Tears of mortification and jealousy were streaming down his cheeks. Meanwhile, I was enjoying every minute of it.

"I—I can't believe it... Issei is living with a blond-haired beauty...? It's absurd... It's unnatural..." Motohama adjusted his glasses with a trembling hand. He, too, was clearly distraught. His whole body was quaking where he stood.

"S-so does Asia wake you up in the morning?!" Matsuda asked pitifully.

"Hmm. You did have to wake me this morning, didn't you, Asia?"

"That's because you're such a sleepyhead, Issei," she answered with a light chuckle.

Matsuda fell backward to the floor.

"Does she serve your meals, too...?" Motohama inquired with trepidation.

"Mom did say you were pretty thoughtful, didn't she?"

"Oh... You're making me blush," Asia said, raising a hand to her cheek.

I watched on cheerfully, my heart filled with a warm and generous feeling.

Motohama glared back at me from behind his glasses, his eyes so sharp, they looked like they would start to cry beads of blood.

Jealousy sure could be terrifying. My whole life, it seemed, had undergone a sudden reversal. Everything was now joyful and rosy, all because I had befriended a beautiful young lady.

Yep, even if the other girls in my class all hated me, so long as I had Asia by my side, nothing else mattered.

No, I reminded myself. *I can't stop here.* My goal was to earn a noble title, become a great demon, and make countless beauties into my loyal servants.

I was going to need other girls who liked me. The trouble was, I wasn't exactly on good terms with most young women...

"Issei! You sure know a lot of cute girls, don't you?! Rias! Himejima! That's both of Kuou Academy's Two Great Ladies! Plus, I've seen you with the petite idol Koneko! As if that wasn't enough, you've snatched up our blond transfer student Asia, too? What gives?! This is totally unfair!" Matsuda cradled his head in his hands.

It was admittedly a little upsetting to see my friend so distraught.

There was nothing to refute, though. I had befriended a good number of beauties over the past month or so.

I was accompanying Asia on her way to school, and both Rias and Akeno seemed pretty fond of me...

Yep, things had finally turned around for me. There was no mistaking that. I was certain these days promised to be the most enjoyable time of my life, and I was going to ensure that I relished them without regret.

While I was considering such things, Motohama calmly adjusted his glasses. "Issei, I'm sure it wouldn't hurt you to introduce us to even one of your new friends. Come on—help us meet someone. Please. I'm begging you." He pushed his face close to mine. His voice was low, but it was filled with intensity.

The only girls I knew were the ones he and Matsuda had already mentioned. In other words, I wasn't acquainted with any others. Heck, I was sure no one else would even take me seriously.

Perhaps that sounds a little harsh, but it was the truth. To put it bluntly, I didn't know any human girls. All the ones I was getting on so well with were demons. Still, demons could be cute, too, so I didn't take much issue with that.

Hmm... After thinking for a moment, I remembered that I did know someone else. Sort of. It was an idea, at least.

I took out my cell and searched through the address book. Sure enough, there it was. This could work.

"Hold on a second."

I left Asia and my two buddies alone for a moment and went to a corner of the room so I could check with the person I had in mind as to whether it would be all right. We spoke on the phone for a couple of minutes, and they were okay with it.

"Everything's good. I know someone who wants to meet you. They'll bring a friend, too. Here's their number and their e-mail address. You should probably get in touch by e-mail or text first. That'll help things move along more smoothly."

"Thanks!" Instantly recovering from his wailing despair, Matsuda snatched my cell phone out of my hand.

Hey, come on—that was a quick turnaround! A second ago, you were crying your heart out!

The two of them copied the number into their own phones.

"Thank you, Issei! We're in your debt! I'll never forget what you did for us this day!"

"Yeah! Let's all go on a triple date! Just you wait! We'll have girl-friends in no time!"

The two of them were grinning in excitement. It looked like they were gorging themselves on happiness, or maybe their minds had been opened to a world of possibility?

"So what's she like? She's cute, right?" Matsuda inquired, hoping to learn more about the person whose number I'd just given him.

I scratched my cheek. "Ah, well, they're definitely a maiden. There's no doubt about that."

"'*A maiden*'…! W-wonderful… Awesome, Issei!"

"I bow my head to you, Master Hyoudou!"

These guys really could be ridiculous at times. Their attitudes had done a complete one-eighty. Who's to say I wouldn't have ended up the same way if I'd never met Rias and Asia, though?

Silently, I whispered an apology for hogging all the fun.

Matsuda, still grinning, glanced back at me. "Hey, Issei. By the way, is it just Mil? What's with that name?"

That was a question Matsuda was going to have to answer on his own. Not even I knew the truth of it.

—○●○—

Pedaling my bicycle at full throttle, I rocketed through the neighborhood at night.

"Hyaaah!" I screamed, putting everything I had into propelling myself forward.

Stopping at our destination, Asia, sitting behind me, popped a leaflet into the mailbox.

"It's done."

"All right!"

After making sure that she was secure behind me, I took off again.

The little ads that Asia and I were distributing were actually simple tools used for summoning demons like us. Normally, a would-be client would've had to draw a magic circle to summon one, but in the modern age, few people were willing to go to such lengths. Actually, it was more that very few people believed such creatures even existed anymore. Until recently, I definitely hadn't.

This left demonic commerce in a bit of a tough spot. To counteract this, flyers complete with their own premade magic circles had been printed.

Each Familia emblazoned their handouts with their own insignia and added different fancy catchphrases that really gave them the look of any other everyday junk mail.

The leaflets probably didn't mean much to those who were already living satisfying lives, but they were enchanted with a special charm that tempted those possessed of raging, unfulfilled desires into using them.

When a client used one, a demon would appear out of the magic circle and grant them a wish in exchange for payment. That was the contemporary way of summoning a demon.

Distributing these leaflets was the number one job for newbie servant demons like Asia and me. Basically, we would start at the bottom for a time and learn the ropes of the trade. We had a special mobile device that helped us identify the homes of those with unquenchable desires. Following the little detector, we would arrive at their place and toss one of the flyers into their mailbox. Then we would move on to the next potential client, rinse, and repeat.

Technically, I had already graduated from this kind of work. I was still doing it only because...

"...Issei, are you sure about this? Helping me deliver these papers, I mean?"

"It's no problem."

Yep, I was there to help Asia. Basically, I was ferrying her by bicycle from one house to the next.

"You don't know how to ride by yourself, right? Someone else pedaling is the only way this'll work."

"I-I'm sorry. I've never ridden a bicycle before... But I can walk—"

"I can't let you do that. I'd worry about you, Asia."

That was the truth. It wasn't so much about whether she could ride by herself but rather that it would be irresponsible of me to let her wander an unfamiliar neighborhood alone.

Asia had arrived in Japan from the northern European countryside only last month. She still didn't know much about the local customs. Her new demon abilities allowed her to speak and understand Japanese, but adapting to an entirely different kind of daily life was another matter entirely. I'd been trying to teach her, but there was still so much left to cover.

On top of that, Asia was too friendly and pure-hearted. There was no telling what kind of trouble she would get herself into.

After giving it some thought and being unable to stop myself from worrying, I'd told the prez that I would help Asia with distributing the leaflets.

Rias graciously agreed to my request.

That's how I'd wound up carrying Asia on my bike from one place to the next each night.

"See that, Asia?" I motioned to an approaching structure. "That's a Shinto shrine. We're demons, so we can't go inside."

"Yes. Demons aren't allowed to enter places where spirits gather or spots that have a connection to God, right? As a Christian, it's hard to imagine eight million gods, though..."

Raised in a monotheistic culture, Asia was unlikely to adapt easily to Japanese religious beliefs, or so Rias had told me.

That was why I'd thought it would be a good idea to use this opportunity to teach her all about her new home.

"Ah! Look over there. It's closed right now, but that bakery makes some great bread. How about I take you there sometime?" I offered.

"Okay! I love Japanese bread! It's so sweet!" Asia replied cheerily.

Even light conversations like this were fun. It was like we were on a nighttime date. What more could I have asked for?

I had always wanted to cycle around with a girl riding on the seat behind me.

"Issei, have you ever seen the movie *Roman Holiday*?" Asia suddenly asked.

"*Roman Holiday*"? *Ah, right, that's a pretty famous one.*

"It's an old film, yeah? Sorry, I haven't seen it," I replied.

"Oh..." Asia sounded a little disappointed.

"What about it?"

"...I love that film... Whenever I saw the characters riding around on bicycles...I always wanted to try it myself..." She paused there, giggling softly. There was a genuine happiness about her, and I felt Asia's arms tighten around me slightly.

I didn't really know what she was talking about, but that was fine. If she was happy, that was enough for me.

The night breeze felt good as we raced along.

"We're back!"

Once Asia and I had finished distributing the leaflets, we made our way to the clubroom.

The Occult Research Club was based in the supposedly unused old school building at the back of the campus. One of the empty class-rooms on the third floor had been adapted into the meeting place and headquarters of Rias Gremory's Familia.

"Oh dear, you both look exhausted. I'll make you some tea." Akeno Himejima, the club's vice president and Rias's number one adviser, was the first to greet us upon our return.

Akeno was a third-year student, which made her my senior. She had a classical Japanese charm, with lustrous black hair and a broad, welcoming smile. She also regularly sported a ponytail, a rare sight in this day and age.

Together, she and Rias were known at our school as the Two Great Ladies. They held the adoration of boys and girls alike at Kuou Academy.

"How was your date?" The next to speak up, flashing us a cool smile, was Yuuto Kiba, the handsome prince who'd captivated countless girls here at Kuou. He was a pretty boy, a real smooth-talking lady-killer. That quality of his made him my mortal enemy.

"Awesome, of course." Regardless of my dislike, I gave him a thumbs-up as I replied.

"...A late-night tryst...," a cold, cool voice observed. Such a sound could belong only to Koneko Toujou, a petite first-year student. At a glance, she looked like she belonged in elementary school. Perhaps that's why she'd become a sort of mascot for our school.

Asia and I approached Rias, who was sitting on the sofa at the back of the room. Her crimson hair was as stunning as ever.

"Prez, we're back," I stated, but Rias kept staring off into the distance.

Perhaps she's got something on her mind? I wondered. It could've been my imagination, but it looked like she let out a small sigh.

Asia, standing by my side, tried to follow Rias's gaze.

"Prez, we're back!" I repeated, louder this time.

With that, Rias snapped back to her senses. "S-sorry. My mind must have wandered. Good work, Issei, Asia."

It seemed to me like Rias was frequently getting distracted lately. While she handed everyone their orders with her usual level of elegance and grace, I did notice her staring off into space a lot. Sighs slipped from between her lips with increasing regularity, too.

Whatever was troubling Rias was likely something I couldn't even hope to guess at. She was a high-class demon, after all. That must have come with its own challenges and issues.

In any event, these were the members of the Occult Research Club. In other words, the students in the club formed Rias Gremory's Familia. Apart from me, everyone else was super-popular at school. Although I suppose I was famous in my own right as a pervert. It wasn't quite the same, though.

Rias looked Asia over. "Well then," she began, "it's time you made your debut."

Huh?! Seriously?!

"Eh?" Asia was clearly confused herself.

"Asia, this means you're a full-fledged demon!" I cried ecstatically. "You'll jump through the magic circle and make a pact with your client!"

"M-me?" she asked, flustered, pointing at her own chest.

"I'm right, aren't I, Prez?" I asked.

"Indeed. I think you've handed out enough leaflets. If I don't put a stop to it now, these dates of yours could get out of hand."

Wha—?! Quit joking around like that, Prez! You're going to embarrass me!

Just as when I'd graduated from flyer duty, Rias drew the magic circle of the Gremory Familia on the palm of Asia's hand. With that mark, she would be able to warp back and forth through the magic circle.

"Akeno, please check that Asia has enough demonic power to make the jump."

"Of course, President."

At Rias's instruction, Akeno placed her hand on Asia's forehead. A faint light began to issue from her fingertips, as if she was gauging something.

"After what happened with Issei, we'd better make sure you're ready. I don't think you'll have a problem, though." Rias's words dampened my spirits.

Still, there was nothing I could've said back. My first real outing as a demon hadn't gone at all to plan. It took only a tiny amount of demonic power to use a magic circle, but I'd been unable to muster even that much.

As unprecedented as it was, I'd been forced to travel to my clients by bicycle. Even now, I still had to pedal my way to people who summoned me. It was humiliating.

"She's fine, President. There shouldn't be any issue. Actually, after you and me, she possesses the most power of any member of your Familia. She has immense latent potential."

Rias broke into a smile at Akeno's report. "That's good to hear. She'll be able to put her Bishop abilities to full use, then."

By *"Bishop,"* Rias was referring to Asia's role as a demon.

Present-day demons gave their servants roles based on the human game of chess. The head of the household was the King, beneath whom served their Pawns, Knights, Bishops, Rooks, and Queen.

This system, known as Evil Pieces, was how members of a demon's Familia were organized.

A short while back, I'd learned from Rias and the others how the system had come about. Many demons had perished in the Great War fought against the forces of God and the fallen angels. The Evil Pieces system was devised as a way of increasing the fighting potential of smaller forces to help balance the odds.

Each piece had its own special attributes, which helped bolster a demon's innate abilities.

Naturally, Rias had assigned such roles to each of us, too.

Akeno was her Queen, Kiba her Knight, Koneko her Rook, Asia her Bishop, and I was her Pawn.

The Pawn might seem incredibly underpowered to the untrained eye, but a Pawn could take down a King when used correctly. Or so Rias had told me. If I was going to work toward becoming the mightiest of Pawns, I had to have faith that such a thing was true.

Anyway, since Asia evidently had plenty of power to spare, it sounded like she wasn't going to have any trouble using the magic circle.

Yep, her future sure looked rosy. I was happy for her.

I was confident that she would get along well with her clients, but that's when I was stung by a pang of unease.

...Asia was extremely kindhearted and naive. What would happen if she was summoned by some sketchy weirdo...?

Case 1

"Whoa! What a cute little demon! Oh, I know! Show me your panties! Flash me your breasts!"

That could be bad..., I thought.

Case 2

"Beautiful demon! Let me fondle your breasts in exchange for my life!"

Would Asia really...? I gulped.

Case 3

"I'll give you my soul—just let me sleep with you tonight!"

I didn't even know what I'd do if someone said that to her.

......

"...Issei, are you crying?" Rias peered at my face, her expression one of concern.

"You can't, Prez!" I shook my head from side to side, tears streaming down my face.

I'd changed my mind; this was no good at all! This was Asia we were talking about! If some unknown client ordered her to do anything indecent, she wouldn't be able to refuse!

She was too hardworking, too earnest! A girl like her was going to do her best to finish the job, even at the expense of herself!

"Prez!" I cried out. "You can't let Asia go alone! I'm worried about her! I couldn't live with myself if some sick perv forced her to do lewd stuff!"

"Issei," Rias began, her expression troubled. "The House of Gremory doesn't respond to summoners whose thoughts toward members of this Familia are too lecherous. We do occasionally get clients like that, but we have someone who specializes in dealing with those cases. I wouldn't put Asia in that sort of predicament. Don't worry—I know what I'm doing."

"Really?! You're sure?! But I'm still really stressed about it!"

Rias let out a tired sigh at my display of concern. "Very well. I'll let you assist her, at least to begin with. How does that sound?"

"Th-thank you! Asia! Leave the pervs to me! All you have to worry about is making the normal contracts!" I took her hands in my own and breathed out a sigh of relief.

"O-okay..." Asia herself looked a little uneasy, as though she thought this was making more trouble for me. Truthfully, I didn't care. I had to protect her. Not only had I promised Rias I would do so, but I was legitimately worried for Asia.

Perhaps you could've said I was being too protective, but I wanted to watch over Asia until she felt confident enough to say that she could handle taking clients all on her own.

I would protect her until she grew tired of me—even if it meant that she started to resent me a little.

"In that case, once you receive a request, Asia, you will be able to jump through the magic circle, taking Issei with you," Rias explained.

"I understand, President," replied Asia.

At that moment, the large magic circle on the floor of the room began to glow.

Akeno, who was in charge of operating it, read the demonic text that appeared on one side of the circle. "Oh dear. Even Asia ought to be able to handle this one."

Hearing the report, Rias broke into a grin. "How convenient. Asia, use your powers to jump straight to the client. Issei might not be able to make the jump by himself, but you're strong enough to bring him with you. Good luck."

I was supposed to be helping her, but in reality, I was the one who needed the hand-holding...

It didn't matter. I was going to protect Asia in my own way.

"Let's go, Asia!" I said.

"Yes, Issei!" she answered.

Thus, the two of us eagerly walked into the center of the magic circle.

—o●o—

It was past midnight by the time Asia and I finally made it home. Her first job had gone surprisingly smoothly, a stark contrast to mine.

"Thank you for letting me shower first," Asia said before heading to the bathroom. Having completed her first contract without any hitches, she seemed unable to stop smiling.

I went back to my room and tried to get some rest. Just like every other night since I'd been made a demon, I was completely exhausted in both mind and body.

After finishing with Asia's client, the two of us had returned to the clubroom to report on her success and finish up for the day. Something about the prez's expression had caught my eye. Again, she'd had that distant look in her eyes, almost as if she was troubled by something.

Worrying about Rias was all fine and good, but I still had to be sure I took my shower once Asia was finished.

Using the same bath as she did... I knew I shouldn't be thinking such dirty thoughts, but I was in the prime of my adolescence. I had to admit, it did make me feel pretty aroused.

No! No, no, no! I shook my head from side to side, trying to dispel my perverted imaginings.

My job is to keep her safe! How low am I that I'm thinking such lewd things about her?! I'm a pervert! An absolute creep! I scolded myself, wishing that I had a hermit's sense of worldly detachment.

Lowering myself to the floor, I crossed my legs to assume a zazen position; then I closed my eyes and tried to empty my mind of all thought.

I told myself that I wasn't a pervert and that I would suffer no more dirty thoughts. I was Asia's protector. I might have been living with her, but it was wrong of me to think of her that way. I recited the Buddhist invocation "Hail Buddha of Infinite Light."

Ow! I was struck by a sudden headache. For a moment, I wondered what had happened. Then I remembered that I was a demon. Reciting sutras could've dealt me some serious damage. Had I kept going, I might've killed myself!

Damn it, I swore. *This is just adding insult to injury!* Then I paused for a moment as I wondered what I was actually trying to accomplish.

Flash!

At that very same instant, the floor of my room suddenly burst into a familiar pattern of light. It was the mark of our Familia!

There was no mistaking a Gremory magic circle. But who was jumping here? And why?!

The light of the magic circle filled the entire room, and a figure took shape at the center of it. Squinting at the light, I spied a feminine silhouette and then brilliant crimson hair…

"Prez…?"

Appearing from within the magic circle was none other than Rias herself. For what reason could she have possibly warped directly to my room?

Somehow, she still looked preoccupied, just as she had back in the clubroom. She looked me over before edging closer. Then she said something completely unexpected: "Issei. Hold me."

…Huh? My mind went blank. What was going on? Had I misheard?

Seeing my bewildered expression, Rias tried a more direct approach. "I want you to take my virginity. Immediately."

I don't think I'd ever heard more stimulating words spoken in my life.

Life.2
I'm Picking a Fight!

"Come on—get into bed. I'll be ready in a moment." Rias all but pushed me across the room as she began to remove her uniform.

H-hold on! What?! My thoughts simply couldn't keep up with her actions!

Whoosh!

She pulled her skirt away, revealing her underwear. Her pure-white panties were dazzling! The shape of her legs was breathtaking! Her luxurious thighs simply begged to be caressed!

Next she reached for her blouse!

"P-Prez! Th-this is…!" I was losing my mind! How could I not be?! Anyone, let alone a sex-obsessed teenager like me, would have been flustered if the prez had suddenly appeared in front of them, saying stuff like *Let's have sex* and taking off her clothes!

Whoosh.

Off came her blouse! I—I could see her bra delicately cradling her breasts! My eyes were glued to her heaving chest!

Wearing no more than her underwear, Rias took a deep breath and then walked toward me.

"Issei. Am I no good?" she asked.

"Th-That's not true at all! I couldn't dream of anyone better!" I hurriedly replied.

"I've put a lot of thought into it, but I can't think of any other way," she said.

Any other way of what?! I had no idea what she meant!

"Once it's done, no one will be able to say anything otherwise. You're the only person close to me who I can do this with."

Me?! I wasn't entirely sure what was going on, but had Rias really chosen me to be her first?!

This was an honor! Or at least that's what I wanted to say, but I couldn't form the words!

"...Yuuto would be no good. He's a Knight to his core. He would refuse. I have to choose you, Issei."

I beat Kiba?! Bwa-ha-ha! I might not have known what was going on, but that was something to be proud of! Victory was mine, you damn pretty boy!

"...You're still lacking in a few areas, but you have true potential." Rias stroked my cheek with the tip of her finger.

My skin was tingling, and my heart trembled with excitement. Some unknown energy was coursing through my body.

"You're the only one who would agree to this immediately after I asked."

"P-Prez..."

Rias drew closer to me and pushed me down onto the bed. She climbed on top and straddled my waist. Her buttocks and thighs were pressing against my you-know-where!

Her crimson hair traced gentle lines across my body. The scent of those brilliant locks was pure bliss.

Snap!

My ears caught the sound of her bra being unhooked. It was the second coming of her glorious, naked breasts! Their beautiful pink tips were already standing erect.

With Rias's every movement, her bountiful bust bounced and swayed. Its destructive power was simply too great!

This was only my second time seeing bare breasts, and both occurrences had taken place in this very bed!

"This is your first time, isn't it, Issei? Or have you done it before?" Rias asked.

"I-it's my first!" I replied nervously.

"I thought so. Me too. We might both lack experience, but let's make sure we see this through to the end. Don't worry—it's very simple. You just need to put it in here." She reached down to touch below her abdomen.

I was so turned on, I felt like my brain might explode at any moment! Next, she took my right hand, and…!

Jiggle.

My hand, guided by Rias's own, squeezed her supple flesh! A soft, warm sensation seeped into each of my fingers! Every nerve in my body was concentrated on that hand!

Gah! I could feel the blood gushing from my nose.

Long had I dreamed of this wonderful impression! I felt like my head was going to burst! If I had to describe the feeling, it was like kneading a high-quality pudding that could hold its shape even after being squeezed! Or maybe a gourmet marshmallow! No, no, even that description wasn't doing this situation justice! Words weren't enough!

"Can you tell?" Rias cooed. "I'm nervous, too. Can you feel my heart beating?"

Now that she mentioned it, I could feel her heart racing beneath her soft bosom. Looking carefully, I could see that her pale-white skin was starting to turn pink.

…*R-Rias is nervous, too?* She was normally so composed and elegant, but I guess even she would feel anxious during her first time.

Without waiting for me to respond, she started to undo my clothes. I was being stripped naked by a girl!

"S-still! I—I don't really have much confidence!" I was so nervous that my voice came out as a high-pitched whine. There was nothing I could've done to help it anyhow. Seriously, I was a virgin!

Rias brought her face closer to mine. "Are you trying to embarrass me?" she whispered.

Pop!

Those words were enough to blow a hole in my consciousness. That was the sound of all my reason and self-control leaving me.

I seized Rias by the shoulders, pushing her down on my bed.

To think that there was a fully naked girl lying beneath me was almost inconceivable. She had said that I could do it with her, though.

Ready yourself, Issei Hyoudou! I thought. While it had all been incredibly sudden, my time had come at last!

No... I began to wonder. *Is this really okay?* Still, a popular, gorgeous older woman had asked me to; there was no way I could resist!

I gulped, catching my breath. Just as my body began to lean against hers...

Flash!

The floor in the center of my room lit up once again. *Who is it now?!* I thought.

Rias glanced toward the light and let out a sigh. "...I guess I was too slow..."

She stared sullenly down at the magic circle. The insignia was, yet again, that of the House of Gremory.

But who could it be? Regardless of whether it was Kiba, Akeno, or Koneko, this was a bad situation for someone to walk in on!

Against all expectations, the one who emerged from the magic circle was an unfamiliar silver-haired woman wearing a maid outfit.

Hold on, a maid outfit?!

She took in the scene of Rias and me on the bed. "Are you trying to break your agreement, Lady Rias?" she asked coolly.

Rias raised an eyebrow. "This is the only way Father and Sirzechs will listen."

"His Lordship and Master Sirzechs will both be disappointed to hear that you gave your chastity to a lowly servant like this."

"His Lordship"? "S-Sirzechs"? *Who on earth are they?* Based on what Rias had just said, maybe the maid meant her father and some other relative? An elder brother perhaps? Did that mean Rias had siblings?

Hold on, "lowly"...? That's me she's talking about, right? Had this maid lady really formed such a poor opinion of me that quickly?

Rias's expression turned sour. "My chastity is mine to do with as I please. What's wrong with giving it to a man of my choosing? And don't you call my cute little servant names. I won't spare you my wrath, Grayfia."

P-Prez...! I'm touched that you would stand up for me!

The woman, apparently named Grayfia, picked up Rias's bra. "In any event, you are the heir of the House of Gremory, so please don't go carelessly exposing yourself to random gentlemen. That applies even in the best of situations." With that, she fitted the bra back onto Rias's body.

The woman turned toward me and bowed her head. "How do you do? My name is Grayfia. I serve the House of Gremory. Pleased to make your acquaintance."

She introduced herself with formal politeness. I'd been taken aback when I had first seen her, what with her insulting me, but now that I got a good look, it was clear that she, too, was a beautiful woman. If she were a human, she probably would've been in her early twenties.

She came off as a calm and coolheaded person, but with her radiant silver hair plaited into three braids knotted together and her gleaming argent eyes, she was a sight to behold. *Grayfia, huh? Maybe I have a thing for older women, too... Owww!*

As I partook of the sight that was this lady in a maid outfit, Rias pinched me on the cheek. I hope the prez knew how much that hurt!

"Grayfia, did you come here of your own volition? Or did someone send you...? My brother perhaps?" Rias wore an annoyed frown. It seemed a fitting expression for a girl her age, but I'd never seen this side of her before.

"All of the above," Grayfia replied.

Rias breathed a deep, resigned sigh. "I see. You, my brother's Queen, came to the human realm personally. So that's how it is. I understand."

She started to gather her clothes. Threading her arms through her sleeves, Rias buried her marvelous nakedness...

"I'm sorry, Issei. Please pretend that this never happened. I wasn't thinking clearly tonight. Let's put it all behind us."

Just like that, it was over. I suppose I never really had any idea what was going on in the first place... Somehow, I knew I was going to regret this later, though.

"Issei? Don't tell me this is him?"

Huh?

Grayfia looked at me with a startled expression. It was quite the revelation to know that even coolheaded women like her could be taken by surprise.

"Yep, Issei Hyoudou," I said. "I'm a Pawn. And the user of the Boosted Gear," I said.

"...The Boosted Gear... You're the one possessed by the Red Dragon Emperor?"

Had something changed? All of a sudden, the maid lady was staring at me as if I were some strange rarity.

"Grayfia, what do you say we go to my stronghold?" Rias suggested. "We can speak there. You don't mind if Akeno joins us, I hope?"

"The Vestal of Thunder? I don't mind. There's nothing unusual about a high-class demon having their Queen by their side."

"Good. Issei?" Rias called as she sauntered over. She brought her face to my cheek and...

Peck.

The touch of her lips against my skin...

Whoa. Whhhhhoooooooaaaaa! A kiss on the cheek?!

"Please forgive me for tonight. I'm sorry for bothering you. I'll see you tomorrow in the clubroom."

With that farewell, she and Grayfia disappeared in the light of another magic circle.

Now alone in my room, I stood dazed. I brought a hand to my cheek, the soft touch of Rias's kiss still lingering.

"Issei!" came Asia's voice a short time later. "You can use the shower now!"

—o●o—

The next morning, Asia and I made our way to school at the usual time.

I rubbed my eyes. I hadn't been able to get any sleep whatsoever.

Damn it. Damn it all!

I knew I was going to regret what had happened with Rias! I'd spent the whole night writhing in agony in my bed!

That warm, soft sensation of Rias's breast lingered on my hand, and the sight of her naked body was engraved into my vision. My whole being had been taken by those memories!

Obviously, this left me with no choice but to do all those perverted things by myself throughout the night! The whole night through! I had to do something to bring my burning lust under control, what with how it had all ended just moments before the main event! Unfortunately, that had now left me completely dejected!

"Are you all right?" Asia asked me worriedly.

The way her pure, innocent eyes stared up at me just made me feel even more dirtied.

I'm sorry, Asia, I thought. *I tried to do something while you were gone that I can't tell you about.* There was no way I could admit that the prez had appeared in my room wanting to sleep with me.

"You didn't do any training today. You aren't hurt, are you?" She really did look deeply worried.

I'm so sorry, Asia…

My usual session had been canceled. I had received a message from Rias earlier that morning saying that the regular practice had been called off for the day.

Well, I was hardly in a state to do it anyhow, especially not with Rias…

My legs carried me unsteadily to the gate and from there to my classroom, when…

"Issei!"

Matsuda was storming down the corridor toward me, his expression one of rage and indignation.

Oh shoot, that's right!

"Diiiiie!"

Motohama was approaching at high speed from the other direction.

They were getting ready to hit me with a lariat coming from both directions. There was nowhere for me to run!

Thump!

Ugh! They caught me in a double lariat, the both of them wrapping an arm around my neck and dragging me to the ground. Damn those two!

I raised my hands to my neck, gasping for breath.

"What the hell?!" Matsuda wailed.

"Issei! You bastard!" Motohama grabbed me by the collar, his eyes burning with murderous intent.

"Come on! What's with you guys?" I blurted, trying to pretend like I didn't know what they were talking about.

That wasn't nearly enough to placate their anger, however.

"Quit screwing with us! What the hell was that?! He looked like one of those goons from a fighting manga! And he was wearing a gothic Lolita dress! Was that his ultimate weapon or something?!" Matsuda screeched as he bawled his eyes out.

It sounded like the two of them had followed up on the number I had given them.

Yep, the shock of meeting Mil must have been too much for them.

Mil was a regular client from my demon work. She was a girl at heart trapped in the body of a legendary strongman. One who dreamed of becoming a magical girl. Her most charming characteristics were her gothic Lolita outfits and the cat ears she always wore.

You might think that this explanation doesn't make much sense, but it's the truth.

All I could say was that she undoubtedly had the heart of a maiden and the machismo body of a professional wrestler.

"That's not all! He brought some friends along! I don't know what kind of meeting that was, but they looked just like Mil! I was terrified! I thought they were going to kill me!"

Oh? So there's more than one of them...? Just imagining such a scene gave me the chills. Were they mass-produced somewhere or something? The Mil series? I made a note to steer clear of them.

"They kept going on about magic and whatnot! What the hell is *Magical World Selavinia*?! What makes them think I know anything about that?!" Matsuda let out complaint after complaint as he shook my body.

"They kept trying to teach me how to deal with these things called 'Dark Creatures.' Apparently, you can defeat them with some rare powder made by mixing salt extracted from the Dead Sea with some Moonlight Flower that blooms only at night... I would've thought a regular old punch from Mil ought to be enough to kill anything...!" Motohama, too, kept growling as he held my head down.

I guess you could say my friends had just come back from a nightmare.

"What's the problem? At least you know how to deal with a Dark Creature now," I joked.

With that, the two of them unleashed a double brainbuster on me.

—o●o—

"Maybe the president has been worried about family matters?" Kiba suggested as we made our way to the old school building.

Asia and I had met up with the pretty boy on our way to the clubroom, so I had decided to try asking him about Rias's constant state of distraction, but it sounded like he didn't know any more than I did.

"Would Akeno know what's bothering her?" I asked.

Kiba nodded. "She's the president's right-hand woman, so if anyone would know, it'd be her."

Hmm... I knew that it wasn't particularly polite to inquire about the prez behind her back, but given what had happened last night, I *was* worried.

That said, I couldn't tell anyone else about that. There was liable to be quite the uproar if the others found out.

It didn't matter right now anyway. For the time being, I had to do whatever I could to help.

When we arrived at the door outside the room, Kiba broke into a serious frown. "...How could I not have recognized her presence until now...?" He narrowed his eyes.

What is it? I wondered. What could've happened?

I pushed open the door without giving Kiba's expression much thought.

Inside were the prez, Akeno, Koneko, and the silver-haired maid Grayfia! She was looking just as composed as she had been last night.

The prez was plainly in a sour mood. Akeno wore her usual smile, but there was a cold sort of aura emanating from her.

Koneko was sitting quietly on the sofa in the corner of the room. It was clear that she didn't want to get involved with whatever was going on.

The tension was palpable, even with the room devoid of conversation.

"Uh-oh," I heard Kiba murmur behind me.

He, Asia, and I entered the room, but no one called out to greet us.

Asia, no doubt also sensing the strained atmosphere, gripped the edge of my sleeve with an uneasy look. I patted her on the head to silently reassure her.

Rias looked at each of us in turn. "I see we're all here. Before we get started, there's something we have to discuss."

"Perhaps I should explain the situation, Lady Rias?" Grayfia suggested.

Rias raised a hand to stop her. "The truth is—"

But no sooner did she begin to speak than the magic circle in the center of the room let out a flash of light.

Huh...? Someone's jumping to the room? But every member of Rias's Familia is already present. Maybe it's someone else who serves the House of Gremory like Grayfia?

I quickly realized that my assumption couldn't have been further from the mark and that I still had much to learn as a demon.

The magic circle changed from its usual form into an unfamiliar pattern.

It was a crest that didn't belong to Rias's Familia!

"A phoenix," Kiba whispered by my side.

That meant it definitely didn't belong to any member of the Gremory Familia!

Light engulfed the room, and a figure formed from within the circle.

Burst!

Flames erupted out of the insignia, filling the room with roiling heat. Damn, it was hot! My skin was practically letting off sparks!

The silhouette of a man appeared in the flames. As he swung his arm to his side, the conflagration subsided.

"Heh. It's been a while since I last visited the human realm."

This man was garbed in a red suit. He sported it casually; he had no necktie, and the top buttons of his shirt were undone, exposing his chest. Judging by his appearance, he looked like he was in his early twenties.

While possessing well-cut features, he had the aura of a reprobate. Immediately, the man buried his hands in his pockets.

To me, he seemed like nothing more than a guy from a host club. Did that make him a host demon? To top things off, he had that kind of pretty-boy face that always got on my nerves. If Kiba was the epitome of the gentle guy, then this new arrival was the wild type.

He cast his gaze around the room, then broke out in a smirk as it landed on Rias.

"My dear Rias. I came to see you."

…"D-dear"? I thought. Just what kind of relationship did he have with the prez?

Rias stared across at him, her eyes narrowing in suspicion. She certainly didn't look happy to see him.

The pretty boy clearly didn't care about that, though, and continued toward her. "Now then, Rias. Let's go take a look at the venue. The date is all settled, so the sooner we get this over with, the better."

What an inconsiderate jerk… Who on earth did this guy belong to? Kiba said something about a phoenix, but that doesn't…

Then the host guy grabbed Rias's arm, the bastard!

"…Let go of me, Riser." Rias's voice was uncharacteristically low. She flicked his hand away.

Whoa, what a terrifying reaction…! I'd never seen the prez this angry before!

The guy—Riser—didn't seem to mind being brushed off, though. For some reason, his every movement really seemed to agitate me. Before I knew it, I found myself yelling at him. "Hey, you! What's with that attitude? You don't speak like that to a lady!" I warned him sharply.

He turned his gaze to me, looking me over as if I were a piece of trash on the side of the road. Man, he was really starting to piss me off.

"Huh? And who are you supposed to be?" It was clear that Riser was in a bad mood now. His voice no longer held the sickly sweet tones with which he had addressed the prez. There was no way he wasn't looking down on me. His hatred was palpable. Even so, I was going to say my piece.

"I belong to Rias Gremory's Familia! I'm Issei Hyoudou, her Pawn!"

There, I said it! I named myself! What's your next move, you demon-host bastard?!

"Hmm? Okay then," he replied.

...Huh?

Such an indifferent reaction caught me completely by surprise. It kind of hurt. Did this mean Riser wasn't interested in me at all? Fine.

"Anyway, who are you?" I shot back.

For the first time, he seemed genuinely surprised. "...Oh? Rias, you haven't mentioned me to your servants? And here I thought there wasn't a demon alive who didn't know my name. You were reborn as a demon, right? Even so..."

"There was no need to tell them," Rias said acidly.

"Ah, you sound as bitter as ever. Heh..." The guy's smirk shifted into a low laugh.

At that point, Grayfia interceded. "Issei Hyoudou."

"Y-yes?"

"This is Riser Phenex. He is a pure-blooded high-class demon and the third son of the distinguished House of Phenex."

Ah, a high-class demon of the House of Phenex. I guess that meant he had a noble title of his own, then. The name Phenex bore an obvious similarity to a mythical, immortal bird that had something to do with fire. I wondered if perhaps that meant phoenixes were just as real as demons were.

The more important question was, what did he have to do with the prez? Was he a friend? A childhood acquaintance?

Unfortunately, the truth of the matter surpassed even my wildest expectations.

"He is also the fiancé of the next head of the House of Gremory," Grayfia added.

...Huh? "F-f-fiancé"? *Of the next head of the House of Gremory... That means the prez, right?*

"He is engaged to Lady Rias."

...

Eh? "E-e-e-e-engaged"?!

"Whaaaaaaaaaaaaaaaaaaaaaat?!"

My screams filled the room. That bastard was Rias's *fiancé*?!

—o●o—

"Ah, your Queen's tea is delicious," Riser complimented.

"My pleasure." Akeno smiled back at him, but she didn't respond with her usual *oh dear* or gentle chuckle. Something about that reaction filled me with dread...

The prez was sitting on the sofa. Riser was sprawled out next to her with his arm around her shoulder. Rias kept trying to brush him off, but the bastard continued to touch her arm, her hand, or her hair. Despite how uncomfortable the prez was, Riser insisted on acting overly familiar. Seriously, could he be any more of a jerk?!

We, Rias's servants, had been made to sit away from the two high-class demons, reduced to watching on from the sidelines.

Ugh... Just looking at him was enough to tick me off! He kept putting his hands all over her! If his fingers came anywhere near her legs, I was going to pummel him! Didn't he know how much *I* wanted to touch them?!

Well, to be fair, I *had* already touched Rias's breasts. That was a pretty amazing feat in and of itself. I'd experienced that wonderful pleasure before even her fiancé.

Heh-heh, right. Yep. I've seen her naked body, too, twice. Heh-heh. I'm the real victor here! Bwa-ha-ha!

"E-er, Issei." Asia, sitting beside me, wore a confused look. "Did something good happen?"

Clearly, my enjoyment of my victory over Riser had been showing on my face.

"...No lewd fantasies allowed," Koneko whispered scathingly.

I had to wonder if that girl was a mind reader or something.

"Issei, you should at least wipe the drool from your face," Kiba pointed out with his usual refreshing smile as he gave me a handkerchief.

"M-mind your own business!"

Before I could clean my face with my sleeve, Asia wiped it away with her own handkerchief.

"You must be looking forward to snacks and afternoon tea. It's almost time," she said.

Ugh. That carefree smile of hers was gut-wrenching. She probably hadn't even suspected that I was having dirty thoughts.

"Thanks, Asia," I said, but in my heart, I apologized to her with all my soul.

At that very same moment...

"Cut it out!" Rias's furious voice echoed across the room.

When I glanced back, she had risen to her feet and was glaring sharply at Riser.

His smirk was as smug as ever.

"How many times do I have to say it, Riser?! I will *not* marry you!"

"Sure, you've said so before, but that isn't how it works, Rias. You know that. I think you understand just how serious your family's situation is, don't you?"

"Your concern is noted! But as the heir of the House of Gremory, *I* will be the one to decide whom I am to marry! My father, my brother, and everyone else are being too impatient! Besides, they agreed that I was free to spend my time as I pleased in this world up until I graduate from a human university!"

"Sure, you're essentially free. You can go to college and do whatever you like with your servants. But that won't stop your father and your dear brother, Sirzechs, from worrying. They're afraid your House and your very lineage are facing extinction. You know how many pure-blooded demons died in the last war. Even now that it's over, we're still at odds with the fallen angels and the forces of God. It isn't unheard of for once-great families to have their heirs get knocked off in pointless skirmishes with our enemies, and when that happens, the Gremory line will be no more. Knowing that, isn't it natural for two pure-blooded, high-class demons to get together? Even you must realize how important the children of such a union would be."

Rias and Riser's conversation had turned to something beyond my comprehension. As stupid as I might've been, however, even I could tell that it had something important to do with the demon realm.

Rias fell silent at the seriousness of Riser's explanation. Her eyes, however, remained stern.

Undaunted, Riser took another sip from his tea before continuing. "This new wave of demons—reincarnated demons born from humans, like your servants here—may be on the rise these days, but where does that leave us high-class demons, the old guard? Sure, there are those long-standing families who bind their fates with powerful reincarnated demons, and that's fine. We do need fresh blood to survive, after all. But what happens to those of us with pure blood? We can't allow ourselves to die out, can we? That was why we were chosen, you and I. I have two older brothers, so my bloodline will be just fine, but you only have one sibling, and your brother has already left your House. That leaves only you, Rias, to inherit the name of Gremory. If you don't marry, your blood will dry out within a generation. Is that how you want your family's long, vaunted tale to end? Thanks to the war, more than half of the Seventy-Two Pillars have already crumbled to dust. This union is about the future of demonkind."

The conversation really had turned serious.

I recalled that Kiba had mentioned the Seventy-Two Pillars once before.

In the distant past, there were seventy-two clans of noble demons, each in possession of dozens of vast armies. Most, however, had met their end during the war. Rias's was one of those pure-blooded clans that had survived.

All that talk about marriage had really raised my ire, but the situation sounded more complicated than I'd first assumed.

Pure-blooded demons, in other words, were ones like Rias and Riser. Their parents, and their parents' parents, were all pure demon stock. Which I guess made Asia and me reincarnated demons by contrast.

It sounded like a pretty ancient tradition, which likely meant my opinion wouldn't really count for much.

That was fine, though. I was content to go along with whatever Rias decided, but only after finding out what she really wanted, of course.

"I have no intention of destroying my family. And I *will* take a husband," Rias stated.

Riser broke into a broad smile at this declaration. "Ah, I knew you would make the right decision, Rias! Then let's—"

"But I won't marry *you*, Riser," Rias interrupted. "I shall wed whomever I think most appropriate. Even the sole heir of an old, waning lineage has that right."

At this, Riser's mood suddenly soured, his eyes narrowing as he clicked his tongue in anger. "...You realize, Rias, that I carry the name of the House of Phenex on my shoulders, right? I'm not about to let anyone drag that name through the mud. You think I wanted to have to visit this cramped, shabby corner of the human world? Just so you know, I despise this realm. The fire and wind here are filthy. For a demon like me, who commands those two elements, it's intolerable."

Whoosh!

A funnel of flame appeared, twisting around Riser's body. Embers danced through the room.

"I will reduce your servants to ashes and drag you back to the demon realm by force if I have to."

His hostility and malevolence spread throughout the clubroom. All at once, there was a powerful pressure bearing down on me—on all of us.

A cold shiver raced up my spine, and my hair stood on end. This was the killing intent of a high-class demon. It was horrible! My whole body was trembling!

Asia gripped my arm. She, too, was quivering, no doubt stricken by fear. I wouldn't have expected her to be able to withstand this sudden, frightful atmosphere. It was the same sense of uneasiness that had hung in the air when I'd faced the fallen angels. No, this was worse.

Kiba and Koneko weren't shaking, but it was clear they were ready to fight at a moment's notice.

The prez rose to meet Riser, a red aura emanating from her.

Riser's whole body was blazing with fire, permeating the entire room with an intense heat. At such an intense temperature, we would've clearly been reduced to cinders if we let them so much as touch us! Riser's flames felt as strong as Rias's own power!

The prez was stronger than the fallen angel I had defeated... But if this Riser was as powerful as she was, then he had to be pretty formidable, right?

The flames gathering around Riser spread out on either side of him and came to look just like the wings of a bird.

Despite such boiling tension, there was one person who remained unflinchingly serene: Grayfia.

"Lady Rias, Lord Riser, please calm yourselves. I won't be able to stand by if you both keep this up. For the sake of Lord Sirzechs's name and honor, I won't hold back." Grayfia's voice was quiet yet intense.

Rias's and Riser's expressions both stiffened. Grayfia, it seemed, was someone to be wary of.

The flames enveloping Riser's body subsided, and he breathed a deep sigh, shaking his head. "...I don't want to get on the wrong side of the woman lauded as the strongest Queen alive. And I definitely don't want to get into a quarrel with those monsters Sirzechs has in his Familia."

Rias's brother sounded like a powerful figure. I'd never imagined that Grayfia could've been so strong. She didn't come across as menacing at all.

Rias, too, quelled her red aura, and she relaxed her battle posture. By the look of it, the worst had passed.

Seeing that both Riser and the prez were no longer preparing to fight, Grayfia continued. "His Lordship Lord Sirzechs and those from the House of Phenex were well aware that the situation might come to this. To tell you both the truth, these were supposed to be the final discussions. However, everyone suspected that we might not be able to resolve the issue here, so they devised a solution to break the stalemate."

"…What exactly do you mean, Grayfia?" Rias inquired.

"Lady Rias, if you are determined to have your own way, may I suggest that you resolve this by defeating Lord Riser in the Rating Game?"

"—?!" Rias was left speechless by this suggestion. She looked well and truly taken aback.

"The Rating Game"? I knew I'd heard that name somewhere before…

Kiba, perhaps noticing my consternation, explained. "It's a game played between noble demons where they have their servants fight against each other," he whispered to me.

Ahhh, now I remember, I thought. It was basically a contest between two demon Familias, by way of their Pawns, Knights, Rooks, Bishops, and Queen.

Apparently, one's skill at the game had a major influence on a demon's standing in society.

I recalled that demons weren't allowed to play it until they reached adulthood, however, which should've ruled out the prez from participating.

Grayfia, however, soon answered my unvoiced question. "As you know, Lady Rias, only demons who have reached the age of maturity are permitted to enter official Rating Game matches. However, in cases where the entrants are underage, unofficial matches are permitted between two pure-blooded demons. Only, of course, when—"

"When it involves a dispute between the two families concerned," Rias finished with a sigh. "In other words, you're saying that my father and the others decided to settle this through a match in the event that I refused the engagement... Just how much do they intend to meddle in my life?!" She was clearly infuriated.

I could feel her temper bubbling just below the surface. This side of her was truly terrifying...

"Do you refuse to decide this through a match, Lady Rias?" Grayfia asked.

"No. I hadn't expected the opportunity. Very well. Let's resolve this on the battlefield, Riser," Rias said, issuing her challenge.

Riser flashed her an amused smirk. "Oh? You'll bite, then? I've got no problem with that. Just so we're clear, though, I'm already old enough to have played this game properly. More times than I can count, actually. I've clearly got the advantage. Are you okay with that, Rias?" Riser's response was equally provocative.

The prez, however, flashed him a bold grin. "I am. I'll crush you, Riser."

"Good. If you win, I'll go along with whatever you say. And if I win, you'll marry me on the spot."

The two of them exchanged burning, baleful glares. I knew better than to get in the middle of such a fiery exchange.

"Very well. I, Grayfia, hereby acknowledge your decision. Acting as witness for both families, I shall be responsible for the conduct of the match. Do you both agree?"

"Yes."

"Yeah."

Both Rias and Riser responded in the affirmative.

"Very well. I shall inform both families," Grayfia said with a bow of her head.

In mere moments, the situation had really escalated! I was going to be participating in a Rating Game!

Riser glanced my way and fixed me with a smirk. That smug, self-satisfied look of his really got on my nerves.

"Hey, Rias. Don't tell me these guys are your servants?"

The prez raised an eyebrow. "And if they are?"

Riser let out a chuckle, as if he found that fact somehow amusing. "Then this won't take long. Only your Queen, your Vestal of Thunder, comes anywhere close to the level of my servants." With that, he snapped his fingers, and the magic circle in the center of the room began to glow.

The sigil that formed was the same phoenix-shaped one as when he had emerged from it. This time, however, new figures stepped out of the light one after the next.

One, two, three... U-uhhh...

I found myself lost for words at the number of new faces that entered the room.

"Well, this is my cute little posse," Riser said with relaxed confidence.

A Familia of a full fifteen members gathered around him.

Among them were what looked like a Knight in a full set of armor and another who resembled a mage with her face shrouded by a hood.

Riser had a full set of pieces. Just like in a game of chess, a demon could have a maximum of fifteen, excluding themselves as King, of course.

From what I gathered, high-class demons each received fifteen Evil Pieces from the Demon King. By granting those pieces to individuals who they wanted to recruit as servants, a demon could bring others into their Familia.

However, if a person's latent potential was particularly high, it would take more of any one kind of piece to recruit them. Because of that, some Familias ended up with only one Knight or one Rook, for example.

There was actually a case like that among Rias's Familia: me. A demon could recruit, at most, eight Pawns, but due to the special nature of my Sacred Gear, the prez had ended up using every single one of those pieces to resurrect me.

That was why it wasn't unusual for high-ranking demons to have fewer than fifteen servants. In Riser's case, though, he had completely filled his ranks.

It was quite a magnificent spectacle, this demon Familia of sixteen members.

On our side, all we had was our King, our Queen, one Rook, one Knight, one Bishop, and one Pawn—one of each piece.

In other words, it's six against sixteen?! That doesn't seem fair!

Actually, there was something else that had caught my attention about Riser's group. Yep, you guessed it—they were all girls!

The Knight and the Bishop who I'd looked over earlier were both women! And there was one wearing a Chinese dress! And two with animal ears! And two identical girls who could have been twins! And a petite Lolita girl! And two curvaceous older women! And a classical Japanese beauty dressed in a kimono! And another wearing an elegant dress, who could well have been a European princess! And a wild-looking older woman with a sword swung over her back! And another dressed like a dancer! And a suspicious-looking woman wearing a mask that covered half her face!

They were all women, and they were all incredible to behold!

What is this? I thought. *Some kind of beauty corps?!*

Something akin to an electric pulse coursed through my whole body. That Riser bastard had actually done a hell of a job! It was my dream come true—a harem! A high-class demon had actually accomplished my dream!

What a guy... Damn him...

"H-hey, Rias...? Your servant there looks like he's about to start crying," Riser said, staring at me. He looked genuinely startled.

Rias glanced my way before placing her hand on her forehead in consternation. "It's his dream to have a harem. I'm sure your servants there have moved him to tears."

Yep. I couldn't have said it better myself. The sight of my lifelong dream standing directly in front of me was enough to make my tear ducts swell. It was truly a thing of beauty. They were all women.

"Disgusting."

"Master Riser, that guy's gross!"

The girls all flashed me looks of repulsion.

Damn you! Damn you all! I swore silently.

Riser tried to console them, all the while stroking their bodies. "There's no need for that, my darlings. It's only natural for a low-class creature like him to look up to his betters with envy. Let's show him just how passionate we all are." With that, he began to share a tongue kiss with one of his servants right in front of my eyes.

Wha—?! I could hear their tongues moving from over here!

The prez was clearly appalled.

"Mm... Ah..." The girl breathed sensual, erotic moans as she wrapped her leg around Riser's waist.

Damn it, my crotch was involuntarily responding to the spectacle!

"Whaaaaa...?" Beside me, Asia's face had turned scarlet, with steam all but rising from her ears. This scene was likely a lot for her to process.

Riser pulled himself away from the girl, saliva trailing from his mouth, and then he started kissing another of his companions with equal fervor! This was too much. He was seriously already moving on to round two!

Is it actually okay to do this kind of thing with your servants?! Really?! Damn it! My jealousy was rising, but I knew if I worked my way to the top, that would be me one day.

After finishing with the second girl, Riser looked down at me with a belittling smirk.

You'll never be able to do this. That's what it felt like the bastard was saying to me!

"You'll never be able to do this, my low-class friend."

"Don't say what I'm thinking out loud! Damn it! Boosted Gear!" I screamed with envy and rage, holding my left hand up into the air.

With a burst of crimson light, the Sacred Gear in my left arm materialized into a red gauntlet engraved with the insignia of a Dragon. This was the Boosted Gear, the Gauntlet of the Red Dragon Emperor—a legendary and immensely powerful item.

I pointed my finger straight at Riser. "A playboy like you doesn't deserve the prez!"

"Huh? Weren't you just wishing you could be like me?"

Shit, he's got a point...

"Sh-shut up! It's different when it comes to the prez! With an attitude like that, you're going to keep messing around with other women even if you did marry her!"

"Great men are known to have great fondness for sensual pleasure. Isn't that a saying in the human world? Words to live by, as far as I'm concerned. Anyway, I'm close to my servants, that's all. Doesn't Rias dote on you, too?"

I couldn't dispute that, but I didn't like the idea of letting this guy off the hook, either! Maybe this was what it meant to despise someone too similar to yourself. The idea that Riser got on my nerves so much because I was a younger, less experienced version of him was an unpleasant one.

"Great man, my ass! You're just some weird bird guy! A fiery phoenix? Ha! More like a roast chicken!"

Riser's face blazed with fury at my provocation. "A roast chicken?! Y-you lowborn dirt! You've got quite the mouth! How dare you speak to me that way! Rias, is this how you've trained your servants?!"

Rias simply turned away from him. "As if I care."

"You damn roast chicken! I'm gonna use my Boosted Gear to beat you to a pulp!"

I had my awesome Sacred Gear! With the way it doubled my power every ten seconds, I could supposedly charge it to the point that I'd be able to defeat God! As long as I was given enough time anyway.

"Forget about the Rating Game! I'll take you down here and now!"

"Boost!" A deep voiced boomed from the gemstone embedded in the back of the gauntlet. With that, my body swelled with energy!

This is the power that brought down a fallen angel, you jackass!

All Riser did was let out a resigned sigh. "Milla. Take care of him."

"Yes, Master Riser." The girl who spoke was as petite as Koneko with a small, childish face.

She was carrying a long, thin staff. It was the kind that martial artists used, and she spun it around above her head as she readied herself.

Hurting a little girl really wasn't what I'd signed up for. I thought that if I simply disarmed her, she'd—

All of a sudden, my body felt weightless. It was like I was floating through the air.

The next thing I knew, the floor was coming right—

Crash!

A deafening roar filled my ears.

…Ugh… Pain coursed through my body, and I had no idea what'd just happened.

"Gah!" I recoiled as a sudden wave of agony struck my abdomen.

Ow… My stomach? When did she get in a blow on my stomach…?

"Issei!" Asia rushed toward me, placing a hand on my gut. At that moment, a faint green light enveloped me. Asia's gentle warmth washed away the pain.

That was her healing ability at work. The power of her Sacred Gear made Asia capable of curing the ills of even those abandoned by God, like demons.

Due to that ability, though, Asia had been pursued by the fallen angels…

More importantly, though, I puzzled over what had happened to me. It was clear that I'd fallen to the floor. Looking around, I saw the desk that I'd crashed into was half-destroyed, with all its miscellaneous items and decorations scattered across the ground.

When I glanced back to Riser and his group, the girl with the long staff was already stowing her weapon.

Had she hit me? I didn't think I'd ever even seen her move. Did that mean I'd been struck without realizing it? Had she thrown me into the desk…?

Riser strolled my way and leaned over me while I was still sprawled on the floor. "You're weak," he whispered in my ear.

—!

Those words carved a deep wound in my heart.

"That was my Pawn Milla you just fought against. She might be the weakest of my servants, but she still has far more combat experience than you. She's a better demon overall, too. Boosted Gear? Ha." Riser tapped my Sacred Gear with his finger, letting out a derisive snort. "Sure, that might be a formidable, unrivaled Sacred Gear. Used properly, it could probably beat me, the Demon King, or even God Himself. But it's had countless users before you, and none of them has ever been able to take down the Demon King or vanquish God. Do you understand what that means?" Riser sneered in amusement. "It means your Sacred Gear is incomplete, and its users are worthless weaklings who can't handle it properly! You're no different! What is it humans like to say at times like this? Right, *casting pearls before swine.* Ha! That's what you are! A worthless treasure! Rias wasted her Pawn when she made you a demon!" Riser laughed out loud as he patted me condescendingly on the head.

...Damn it! I clenched my teeth in mortification. I wanted to shout something back at him, but no words came. Riser was right. I was weak. I had been soundly defeated by a little girl. I hadn't even been able to see her attack. Never before had I felt so ashamed.

"Still, our match would be more interesting if you did learn how to use it a bit." Riser cupped his chin with his hand, as if striking on an idea. "Rias, how about we have our game in ten days' time? I'm fine doing it right now, but that wouldn't be much fun."

"...Are you giving me a handicap?" Rias asked.

"Does that bother you? Anger and passion are fine, but they won't win you the Rating Game. If you can't draw out your servants' abilities, you've already lost. There's nothing strange about training them up before your first match. No matter how great their potential, no matter how massive their strength, I've seen more demons than I can count lose their first match because they can't put their tools to proper use."

Rias listened on without responding.

When he was finished, Riser pointed his hand at the ground, and the magic circle lit up once more.

"Ten days. Knowing you, that should be enough time to train up your servants." His gaze shifted to me. "Don't disgrace Rias, Pawn. Your strength is her strength."

—!

I knew at once that those words were meant for the prez.

"See you at our match," Riser said in parting as he and his group disappeared in a flash of light.

"...Damn him."

Lying down in my bed, I desperately tried to bring my seething anger and frustration under control.

After the encounter with Riser, Rias had called off our club activities, our demon work, for the day. She had withdrawn into some deeper room of the old school building with Akeno.

Surely, they were holding a strategy meeting. They had to devise a tactic that would ensure our victory during the Rating Game. It was the prez's first match, after all, so of course she would want to spend some time devising a plan.

Ten days...

It was such a short amount of time. I couldn't help but wonder whether we would be able to ready ourselves and work out a way to defeat Riser and his group by then.

Being just a Pawn, there was little I could say that would help now. I'd just had to go and show off in front of the prez and provoke Riser. And all I had to show for it was a butt-kicking delivered by a pipsqueak.

Arghhhhh! Just thinking back on it all made me want to curl up and die from embarrassment! I really was weak.

My eyes fell to my left arm. There was an absolute, potentially unlimited power lurking in there, in that Boosted Gear.

Even with such incredible strength, it had a considerable weakness. Me, its user.

"Pearls before swine" indeed. Riser had been right.

I cursed myself for being so pathetic.

My dream was to become a harem king. Then along came Riser, a demon who'd already made that dream a reality.

What does he have that I don't? I asked myself. The answer was obvious, though. Power. No, maybe it was more than that. There were also his status and his skills to consider. I had none of that.

"Ah, damn it all!" I sat up in bed, clawing at my scalp in frustration.

Rias had said that she didn't want to get married just yet and that she was specifically opposed to wedding Riser. She'd decided to fight him if that was what was needed to break off the engagement.

I might not have known much about high-class demons or about the complicated situation between their families, but I was determined to fight for Rias's sake!

There were a lot of things I owed to that crimson-haired beauty. That's what stirred me to action. I wanted to be there to support her!

With my mind made up, I decided to resume my training tomorrow morning.

Scratch that! I thought. *I'm going to devote the whole day to it!*

I was sure I could get the day off school if I told the prez what I was planning. My next ten days would be spent doing as much preparation as I could.

The thought struck me to ask Kiba about how to use a sword. I could get Akeno to teach me how to use demonic magic, too. Koneko could even be my sparring partner to work on close combat!

Yep! I had set my sights on my goal! Ten whole days of training!

Making clear-cut plans made me feel a little better. All that was left to do for the day was take a bath.

I got ready and made my way down the hall. Still pretty pumped up, I entered the bathroom and stripped off my clothes. The thought occurred to me that I should tell Asia about my idea once I'd finished cleaning myself up.

I pushed the door open when—

"Ah..."

"Wha—?"

Asia and I came face-to-face in the bathroom.

I was stark naked...

And so was she!

There was a blond, naked beauty standing before me! What a glorious turn of fate! No, it was an accident!

Had she been in here the whole time?!

I'd been so preoccupied that I'd completely forgotten to check whether anyone was already in the bathroom!

Asia's body was dripping with water. She must have been taking a shower.

Her blond hair was plastered to her soft, gorgeous white skin. It was incredible.

Her proportions were perfect... A tight waistline and modest, pert buttocks. Asia's thighs were neither too slender nor too thick, the perfect size for my tastes! Were I to ever glimpse those thighs through a slit in a skirt, I would be down on my knees in supplication!

Then there were her breasts. Normally they were hard to make out when she was clothed. They certainly weren't small...not a bad size at all, in fact!

Asia... You're incredible... Ugh, no! I told myself. This wasn't the time to be getting emotional! Why was I still staring at her?!

Damn it! If only I'd had Motohama's Three-Size Scouter ability. This was the second time I'd found myself wishing for that power!

Next time I saw him, I resolved to have him teach me how to measure a girl's sizes by sight alone! Truly, it was a formidable talent. Its usefulness might've even eclipsed my Sacred Gear!

No! I scolded. I had to stop staring!

I was supposed to be protecting Asia! This was a place where she was supposed to be safe! I had made a vow! So why did I have to keep staring, to keep getting aroused...?

......

Uh-oh!

I could see Asia's gaze shift slowly toward my crotch.

No, Asia! Don't look! It's too soon!

"..."

I was too slow to cover myself.

"Eeeeeek!" I was the one who let out that high-pitched scream.

What was I doing? I had literally just shrieked! Sure, having a girl see my privates was embarrassing, but that was a little humiliating.

"—Ah." Asia's whole body suddenly flushed red, and she turned away.

Hey, hey, cover yourself, Asia! I can still see it all! Was glimpsing my you-know-what so overwhelming that she'd forgotten to cover herself?!

As I thought about it, I realized this could've been the first time that Asia, a former nun, had actually seen a man's private parts. It must have been quite a shock for her.

That must have traumatized her! What had I done?!

"I-I'm sorry! I-I'll leave!" I spun around to head back for the door, but Asia grabbed my hand to stop me.

Wh-what is the meaning of this, Asia?! The thought screamed in my mind.

"...S-sorry. I-I've never seen a man's...before... I'm really sorry...," she mumbled, unable to get out every word.

There was definitely no need for her to force herself to say such indecent things.

"N-no, i-it was my fault... I—I should have checked first... My bad, Asia... I didn't mean to stare at you..." I did my best to offer a sincere apology. The fault lay with me, after all. I'd been the one who barged right in without even bothering to check whether anyone was already inside.

Even if the door wasn't locked, I should've knocked first. We had a new family member living with us, after all.

Regardless of how it'd happened, though, the image of Asia's naked body had been forever stored in my memory.

Please forgive me if I summon it up every now and then.

"No, I understand... Everyone has told me about Japan's bathing customs, and I'm...I'm okay with it..." Asia fidgeted nervously.

Huh? I wondered. *T-told her about them? About what exactly?* "Bathing customs"?

"In Japan, I heard it's normal to bathe together n-naked... That you can deepen your relationship with someone by bathing together..."

—!

Who on earth could have told her such a wonderful—no, such a perverted idea?!

Clearly, Asia had misunderstood. Communal bathing *was* a thing in Japan but only between people of the same sex!

Asia's cheeks continued to redden. "...I...I was told that...if I wanted to d-deepen my relationship...w-with someone I cared about... If it's Issei... No, I—I want to deepen our relationship... So won't you bathe with me...?"

Bah! Blood began to pour out of my nose. Nosebleeds were becoming a pretty common occurrence for me.

...Hold on. We're crossing into dangerous territory here, Asia.

I was a guy. Hearing a girl utter those magic words was making my libido skyrocket! I wasn't sure what I might do if we really went through with this.

But Asia trusted me from the bottom of her heart. If I was to show my true colors...

Aaaaarrrrrrggggghhhhh! I couldn't! I mean, I wanted to! But if I did...

Asia was the kind of person who might forgive me even if I forced myself on her!

No! I told myself. I couldn't harm such a pure, innocent soul.

This was the situation that I had long been waiting for! I had been so close to scoring with the prez, and now fate was making a mockery of me. Even knowing that, I couldn't go through with it. Not with Asia. I would just end up feeling so guilty!

Taking her in my arms and surrendering myself to my feelings would've been easy, and I would've been rewarded with absolute ecstasy.

Those actions would have consequences, though. I knew if I made a mistake like that, I'd regret it for the rest of my life.

It might've been okay if Asia and I had reached this level more naturally, but we hadn't.

When I was with Rias, I'd let myself succumb to her advances, but this time I had to restrain myself!

A purely physical relationship would leave us both hurt! Plus, it was my duty to protect Asia. My lust could not be set free; I had to contain it.

Having made up my mind, I turned around to face her. I rested my hands on her shoulders and opened my mouth to reason with her.

Damn, but her skin was so soft!

"Asia! Listen to me! There's something you need to know about communal bathing! I mean, you're a girl, so if a guy enters the bathroom, you need to be ready to defend—"

In spite of my mental disarray, I desperately fought to contain my inner turmoil. I had to tell Asia how to take care of herself if a guy like me wandered in on her.

Click.

At that moment, the door suddenly swung open.

"Asia. I've brought you a fresh towel." My mom had appeared in the doorway.

It looked like she had come to leave something clean to dry off with on the washing machine, but she froze in place upon seeing Asia and me standing naked by the bath.

This wasn't good. No excuse could've explained this away! No matter how you looked at it, what else could she have seen than a young couple about to have sex?!

Mom, moving awkwardly like a robot, closed the door. In a loud voice, she cried, "D-dear! We're going to be grandparents!"

I fled for my bedroom, still completely naked and burying my face in my hands over the shame of it all.

Had I dropped dead on the spot, I would've welcomed the escape.

The next morning, I called Asia to my room. We needed to have a serious discussion, so we sat in *seiza* position, the formal Japanese way of sitting, across from each other.

"Do you understand now, Asia?" I asked after having explained.

"I do, Issei," she replied.

"Men are wolves. They'll devour you if you get too close to them."

"…Is that so? How terrifying… I'll have to make sure I don't go out during a full moon…"

Asia looked to be truly frightened by my analogy. I held my head in my hands. This was all becoming a bit too much of a headache.

After the bathroom incident the previous night, I had to warn Asia of the danger posed by guys like me. She was simply too defenseless. Given that she hadn't exactly lived a normal life, it wasn't particularly surprising to learn that she didn't know how the world really worked.

Without knowing the dangers of guys my age, about how they would prey on girls like her, she wouldn't be safe leading a normal high school life.

If anyone like that came near her, I would beat the crap out of them, but that wasn't enough. Asia needed to have the strength to protect her purity herself.

Though perhaps this was the sort of thing Asia was better off learning from other girls.

After what had happened last night, my parents, overjoyed, had gone to a late-night discount store to buy baby clothes and toys. No matter what I'd said to them, they refused to listen.

"Don't worry—we understand," my mom had assured. "A lot of people don't get married until they've got a kid on the way. You'll be fine. Ah, I sure would love a granddaughter..."

My dad wasn't much help, either, adding things like, "So I'm going to be a grandfather... If it's a boy, I'll have to buy him a carp streamer. I guess we're an international family now. I'll have to learn English."

There was nothing I could do. My family was beyond saving.

At any rate, I needed to make sure Asia held no misunderstandings about teenage boys.

"Not exactly, Asia. Guys like me...teenage guys, we're really interested in girls like you. I don't think it's any exaggeration to say that we think about you every day. We probably all have indecent fantasies every few seconds. If we get to see a girl's panties for just a brief moment, that's a cause for celebration."

"Do you have indecent fantasies, too, Issei?"

"Ah, yeah. I'm a bit of a pervert. You knew that, right?"

"Yes," Asia replied with a broad smile.

That carefree look tore at my heart.

Right, she already knew I was a pervert...

"Y-yeah. That's me. Guys like me are scary, okay? They could talk an innocent girl like you into following them into a dark place somewhere and then do something really bad."

"'*Something bad*'?" Asia tilted her head adorably.

Seriously, her every movement was just too cute.

"Th-they could touch you, and touch you, and touch you some more! They could subject you to some pretty indecent stuff! It's dangerous, okay? You should be afraid of them!"

"Yes, I am. But if I'm ever in danger, I'm sure you'll come to save me, Issei," she answered with a beaming smile, as if she had the utmost faith in me.

I could feel my eyes growing hot. Yep, she really did trust me. I was beyond moved.

This was no time to get sidetracked, though, nor was it the time to get emotional. I cleared my throat. "Still, you're a girl, Asia, so you need to have a better sense of danger and of how to deal with it. I really worry for you sometimes, seeing as how trusting you are of everyone."

"You're worried about me?"

"Yep, I'm terrified. If someone was to do something to you while I wasn't looking, I might end up killing them. That's how concerned I am about you," I answered with the utmost sincerity.

Perhaps because I had raised my voice a little, Asia's expression had become more serious than before, and she listened on in silence.

Those were my honest thoughts. If someone was to ever hurt Asia, I really didn't think I'd be able to hold back, even if the offender was just a normal human. My being a demon and possessing a Sacred Gear meant that a regular person had no chance against me, but I still didn't think I'd hesitate to unleash my fury on anyone who wronged Asia. Even if the prez killed me for it, I would still destroy them. That was how important Asia was to me.

Why, though? Was it because she was a girl? That was part of it. Maybe the reason was that I liked her? I couldn't deny that was a component, too.

More than anything else, however, it was because I'd changed her life forever. It was my fault that Asia, who might've otherwise spent her life as a nun, was now a demon. She had ended up this way all because of my own sense of justice. Or perhaps it'd been my own selfishness. At the time, I had thought that having her become a demon was the best way of helping her, but still…

The prez probably didn't hold it against me. She would likely just say something like, *I was the one who made her into my servant, so you don't need to blame yourself.* Words like that wouldn't change how I felt, though.

I had resolved to watch over Asia, to protect her, so that she could live a happy life. I, Issei Hyoudou, would protect Asia Argento for the rest of my life. Of course, I had a duty to protect Rias, too, but that was a little different.

That was something I couldn't forget about, either.

Protecting the prez. Not only did I like Rias as a girl, I respected her, too. That was why I wanted to watch out for her, similar to how a warrior might've defended their general. I guess you could say that I was like a subordinate dedicated to serving a master whose intent was to conquer the world.

Protecting Asia. I definitely had feelings for her, but if anything, those feelings were closer to wanting to look after a cute younger sister.

That's why I had to drive away any bad person who got too close to her. Then again, seeing as I didn't actually have a sister, there was no way of telling whether that was how older brothers truly felt.

That said, I also wanted Asia herself to get stronger. That way, our future would be one where we'd always be able to laugh and smile together.

"I understand. I won't do anything to make you worry, Issei. I promise. So please, teach me what I need to do."

"Yeah, I know. But I think you would get better advice asking a girl rather than me. Let's talk to Akeno and the prez and see what we can do."

"All right."

"Phew." I breathed a deep sigh.

It sounded like things would be okay. At any rate, I could talk to the other girls in the Occult Research Club about it once I got to school.

That didn't mean I was going to mention the incident in the bathroom, though.

"U-um... Issei, there's something I've been wanting to ask you," Asia suddenly said. Her cheeks turned red, and she fidgeted nervously.

What now? I wondered.

"A-about what happened last night... If it'd been the president instead of me...would you have bathed with her...?"

What...?

I found myself at a loss in the face of this unexpected question. I had never anticipated Asia asking me anything like that. Despite turning a deep shade of red, her expression remained earnest and serious.

Huh? Huh? Why ask this now? Asia's question had knocked me completely off balance.

What does the prez have to do with what happened yesterday? I thought. If it had been her instead of Asia...

Issei, come over here. I'll wash your back for you. Are you nervous? It's all right, my cute little servant—just leave everything to me.

Her slender white fingertips would slide down my back. I could already feel myself getting excited.

Here, turn around. Oh? What do we have here? You might be nervous, but this fellow here is betraying your true feelings. How very like you, Issei.

Her hand would reach between my thighs, and then...

Suddenly, I snapped out of my lewd fantasy, only to find that blood was running from my nose!

If Rias really had said something like that to me, I honestly had no idea what would've happened!

Perhaps I would've asked something like, *Prez, can I wash your breasts?!*

I could imagine her letting me do as I pleased with a magnanimous smirk. Such a powerful fantasy was really too much for me!

I glanced toward Asia, only to find her eyes glistening with tears.

"I was right, wasn't I? It would've been fine if it was the president, wouldn't it? Oh... It's okay. I knew that from the beginning. I did. Really. But still..."

......

She's crying! Asia's crying?! Why?! What for?! I started to panic.

"And what are you two up to?" came a sudden new voice.

I turned around, only to see Rias let out a sigh as she brushed back her crimson hair.

"P-Prez."

"A lovers' quarrel this early in the morning? You two sure are close."

"N-no, th-that isn't...!"

"Come along now—we're going. Make sure you're ready to spend a few nights away from home."

Going? Where? And for a few nights?!

Rias, seeing my confusion, flashed me a smile. "We're going to be doing our training in the mountains."

—o●o—

"Argh..."

I gasped for breath as I hauled a humongous backpack filled with luggage.

"Yo-ho!"

"Yo-ho!"

Someone's voice echoed off in the distance.

Damn you, you show-off hiker! I cursed. *Go and have your fun!*

We were in the mountains. The prez had brought us all there to get us ready for the upcoming match.

After showing up at my house that morning, Rias had made Asia and me pack our things and prepare for a long trip. The others had already used the magic circle to gather at the foot of the mountain.

It was a clear, sunny day. We were surrounded by trees and nature. Chirping birds sang from every direction. The mountain scenery was amazing.

The problem was the incline. With every step I took, it battered my strength. My sweat was running in rivers.

"Come on, Issei! Pick up the pace!" Rias called from much farther up the slope.

Asia was standing next to her, watching me with worried eyes.

"...I'll go help him," she said.

"Don't. If he can't do this for himself, he won't grow stronger."

I could hear the two of them talking.

Thank you, Asia, I thought. *And, Prez, you've got a heart of stone sometimes.*

Seriously, this bag was killing me. It was just too heavy...

Slung over my shoulders was a humongous rucksack. I also had a bunch of other bags hanging from my arms. Not only was I carrying my own things but Rias's and Akeno's as well.

Supposedly, this was all part of my training, but I was sure I was going to die before we reached wherever we were going.

What's in these bags anyway?!

"President, I've gathered some mountain vegetables. We can use them when we cook dinner tonight," Kiba said, passing me by with his overly cool expression.

He, too, was hauling a huge backpack, but I was left speechless when I saw that he wasn't having any difficulty at all with the steep mountain path.

Kiba had even stopped to gather some plants; he was clearly far fitter than he looked.

"...Excuse me."

The next thing I knew, Koneko, hauling an even larger load of luggage, passed right by me! Wha—?! Just where did her Herculean strength come from?! Damn it, I couldn't afford to lose to those two!

"Yearghhhhh!" I poured all my strength into pushing on up the mountain! I was going to bite it! Seriously, my heart was about to give way any minute now!

Things continued like this for a good while, until we finally reached the cottage that was our destination.

From what I'd gathered, the wooden hut belonged to the Gremory family.

It was normally hidden from human eyes, blending into the surrounding scenery thanks to some kind of enchantment. Nonetheless,

now that we had arrived to use it, it had become visible. A distinct woodsy scent crept from somewhere inside.

I entered the living room to set everyone's luggage down, took a mouthful of water, and promptly collapsed to the ground.

The girls went upstairs to the second floor to change into looser clothing.

"I'll go get changed, too," Kiba said, heading for the bathroom on the first floor with a blue sweater in his hand. "Don't try to spy on them," he added half-jokingly.

I wanted to respond, saying something like, *Don't make me punch you!* but I was too exhausted for anything more than a glare.

Seriously, if the girls from school could've seen us, they would've been up in arms. Recently, they'd been spreading rumors about us being a BL couple. *Issei/Kiba or Kiba/Issei* was a hotly debated topic.

The whole *Beauty and the Beast* quality of those rumors had caused them to spread like wildfire through each class. I didn't really understand it all, but it did sound like that meant I was the beast. I cursed all who had spread such lies.

After catching my breath a little, I changed into a fresh pair of clothes in one of the empty bedrooms. The space was furnished with a bed and all the usual everyday necessities, but no television.

By the time I'd finished getting ready, everyone else had already returned to the living room.

Dressed in her red tracksuit, Rias flashed me a grin. "Now then, let's get started."

Life.3
I've Begun My Training!

Lesson 1: Swordsmanship with Kiba

"Yah!"

"Augh! Yargh!"

Kiba and I traded blows with our wooden practice weapons as we began my sword training.

That pretty boy gracefully countered my every attack. No matter how powerfully I swung my blade, he deflected it each time without any apparent difficulty.

Clash!

Once again, he knocked my sword out of my hands.

"No, you mustn't focus only on your opponent's weapon. You need to widen your vision and take in your opponent and his surroundings, too."

Kiba could say things like that all he wanted, but it wasn't that simple. The more we practiced, the more I realized just how wide the gap in our skills was.

Yep, as Rias's Knight, Kiba had skills and techniques that were incredible. Each time, he defeated me with minimal movement. He had much more practice than I, much more combat experience, and, most importantly, much more talent in swordsmanship.

"We're not finished! Here I come!"

That was the day I learned just how formidable Kiba's swordsmanship was.

Lesson 2: Demonic Magic with Akeno

"No, you need to gather your power inward and let the aura flow over your body. Concentrate your thoughts and feel the wave of your energy."

Akeno, dressed in her black tracksuit, tried to explain magic to me, but still I couldn't gather even a paltry amount of demonic force into the palm of my hand.

Urghhhhh... Focus! Concentrate! Visualize yourself gathering your power into your hand!

"I did it!" Asia, wearing a white jogging outfit, had succeeded in gathering a large mass of pale-green light at her fingertips. I supposed it was the color of her demonic energy. It was a beautiful sight.

"Oh dear. Our cute little Asia is a talented one," Akeno praised.

Asia's cheeks turned red.

Urgh... I, on the other hand, was no good at all. I couldn't even make the first letter of the words *demonic power* appear in the air. All my best efforts could muster was a small little sphere the size of a pinprick, but it was like a grain of rice compared to Asia's softball-size mass of force.

I at least took some comfort in knowing that Asia was getting stronger.

I—I mean, I have the most powerful Sacred Gear, after all! Ha-ha-ha!

"Now then, let's try turning that energy into an elemental force like fire, water, or lightning. You need to visualize what you're trying to accomplish, but for beginners like you, it will probably be easiest to start with fire and water."

At that, Akeno poured her energy into a water-filled plastic bottle.

Splash!

Imbued with her demonic powers, the water transformed into a sharp barb and tore the bottle open from the inside out.

Whoa. Incredible, I thought.

"Asia, I want you to try copying what I just did. Issei, you should keep practicing on how to concentrate your powers. The source of your abilities is in the visualization. In any event, it's important to materialize the image in your mind."

Right. Visualize it. Materialize the image in my mind...

"It may be easier to form an image or an idea that is constantly in your thoughts," Akeno added.

That was all well and good, but I wasn't particularly... Wait a moment. There was something I was always thinking about. D-did that mean I could bring my wild fantasies to life?

"Akeno, can I have a minute?"

If I could actually pull off what I was thinking, I was going to be invincible. The idea was pure genius!

Akeno stared blankly at me for a moment after hearing my idea. Then she let out an amused laugh. "That's very like you, Issei."

Whoa! Does that mean it's actually possible?

Akeno went back to the cottage. When she returned, she was holding a pile of onions, carrots, and potatoes in her arms. I wondered if, perhaps, she was making curry or something.

"Now then, Issei. While we're staying here, I want you to handle this job. I'm sure you can strip them all bare."

With those words, I understood exactly what Akeno was asking of me.

It looked like this new path I'd discovered was going to be harder than I'd first expected.

Lesson 3: Sparring with Koneko

"Hiyahhh!"

Thump!

That was the tenth time I had succeeded in getting myself tossed into a tree.

Koneko had sent me flying with a single punch yet again! I didn't know what to do!

"…Weak." The petite, childish girl in a yellow tracksuit had offered only a single biting word for me.

Why does it have to be this way?! I cried internally. My weaknesses had already been made apparent during that fight with Riser's servant. Being thrown around by another little girl was just adding insult to injury.

Koneko specialized in throws, grapples, and other hand-to-hand techniques. Her Rook attributes made her strength and defense absurdly powerful. Her petite body and incredible agility meant that if I took my eyes off her for even a second, she would appear right in front of me and deliver another crushing blow.

It was plain that Koneko was still holding back, but that didn't mean each hit wasn't immensely painful.

"…Aim for the center of the body, and strike like you're trying to carve a hole in them," Koneko instructed. Such a thing was easily said, but for a beginner like me, landing a hit was an entirely different matter.

Swinging her arms around, Koneko aimed another fist squarely at me.

"…Next round."

I was done for.

Lesson 4: With the Prez!

"Hey, Issei! Give it your all!"

"Right!"

I was making my way up another steep mountain path, carrying a boulder tied to my back with a rope. Not only that, but the prez was sitting atop that rock.

She kept ordering me to make my way down the mountain and then back up. The unpaved trail was seriously exhausting.

After several dozen laps, my legs were seriously stiffening up. Rias finally relented. "That's enough," she said. "Next is strength training. We'll start with push-ups."

"R-right..."

Rias was a monster. A monster of a prez!

My basic skills and abilities were so paltry that I was forced to put much more work into improving myself than the other members. Not only that, but Pawns also moved around the battlefield more than the other pieces. That meant that finding a way to increase my strength and stamina was essential.

"Gah!"

Mercilessly, Rias placed the boulder on my back again as I started doing my push-ups. Thanks to her demonic powers, even lifting a huge rock like that was no problem for her. If only she could've done the same with all that luggage I had to carry...

Plop.

"Augh..."

As if weight training with a boulder on my back wasn't bad enough, Rias sat herself atop the large stone. Even that slight increase in weight sent tremors coursing through my body...

"Now then, let's see you do three hundred push-ups," Rias commanded.

"Okay!"

Had I not been a demon, I surely would've died a hundred deaths.

—o●o—

"Whoa! Delicious! This is seriously tasty!"

After a full day of arduous training, we sat down to have dinner together.

The table was adorned with all sorts of luxurious dishes. The herbs that Kiba had picked earlier had been boiled and served with a delicious broth.

There was boar meat, too. Apparently, the prez had hunted it herself. I'd never eaten boar meat before, but it was tastier than I had expected.

Next came the fish. From what I'd gathered, Rias had caught them, too. They'd been salted and roasted over an open flame, but even such simple fare was also a delight.

There were plenty more dishes lined up for us to sample, too.

"Oh dear. We have more than enough for seconds, so eat up," Akeno said as she refilled my rice bowl. She was the one who had prepared everything.

Whoa! Delectable! Seriously scrumptious!

Everyone was helping themselves. Exhausted though I was from all my training, I gulped down one serving after another.

Most of that huge bag of luggage had been an assortment of cooking utensils. The food was so amazing that it had been worth lugging it all up the mountain!

Koneko was, rather surprisingly, stuffing her face with food, but I knew better than to crack a joke about that.

"Akeno, this is incredible! Maybe you should be my wife?" I said.

"My, you're embarrassing me." She smiled, raising a hand to her cheek. The Japanese-style apron she was sporting really suited her.

"…I made the soup." Asia, sitting next to me, suddenly turned sullen. She looked as if she was about to start crying.

She must have been talking about the onion soup. The fact that I'd praised only Akeno's food must have made her feel bad about herself.

Hurriedly, I gulped down a bowl of the soup. Unsurprisingly, it was plenty tasty!

"This is delicious, Asia! Awesome even! Let me have another bowl!"

"Really?! Thank heavens… In that case, maybe *I* could be your…" The blond girl trailed off.

"Huh? I missed the end of that. Your what?" I asked.

"N-no, nothing!" Asia, her face turning scarlet, waved her hands back and forth as if to take it all back.

Huh? What is she trying to say?

"Now then, Issei. What do you think after your first day of training?" the prez asked as she sipped her cup of tea.

I placed my chopsticks down on the table before responding. "...I'm the weakest one here."

"Indeed, there's no denying that."

The readiness of her reply made me want to die.

"Akeno, Yuuto, and Koneko each have plenty of combat experience, even if they have never participated in a Rating Game, so I expect that they will be able to fight once they pick up the rules. But you and Asia both lack practical experience. That said, we can't afford to ignore Asia's healing ability or your Boosted Gear. Your opponents will realize that, too, no doubt. At the very least, I want you to be strong enough to retreat from danger when the need arises."

"Retreat...? Is that so difficult?" I asked.

Rias nodded. "Escape is also a part of one's battle strategy. You need to be able to fall back and correct your formation when needed. That's one path to victory. That said, it can actually be quite difficult to retreat from your opponent. If you are on par with them, you might be able to get away with it. But turning your back on someone much stronger than you is the act of a person with a death wish. That's why knowing how to safely fall back is an important aspect of your overall skill. I will teach you and Asia when and how to retreat. Of course, you also need to learn how to fight face-to-face."

"Understood," I said.

"Me too," Asia added. Now that she'd been resurrected as part of Rias's Familia, she was going to be dragged into this fight, too.

...I needed to have the power to protect her in battle. At the very least, I had to be strong enough to be her shield. My resolution on that front was unwavering.

"There's a wonderful hot spring nearby, so what do you say we take a bath once we've finished our meal?" Rias asked.

At this suggestion, my mind immediately went to places it shouldn't! *A hot spring?! An open-air bath?!*

If that was the case, I might even be able to catch a peek of the others!

Yep, peeking at the ladies was the royal road of open-air baths! As a guy, it was my duty to spy on them!

"I'm not going to peek at the others, Issei," Kiba said, delivering a preemptive punch with that graceful smile of his.

"Idiot! D-don't say it out loud!"

"Oh? Issei, were you planning to spy on us?" Rias asked.

Everyone's eyes fell on me.

Uh-oh. This was bad... I felt like I ought to apologize for being a pervert.

To my surprise, Rias let out a faint laugh. "Then how about we bathe together? I don't mind."

Wha—?!

A bolt of lightning shot through my body. The prez's use of language was as titillating as ever! She could make me weep tears of joy!

"How about you, Akeno?"

"I don't mind bathing with Issei. Maybe I'll offer to wash his back?" Akeno responded with a cheerful chuckle.

She would wash my back for me?! Wait, seriously?! Is that really an option?!

Just how open-minded were the female members of this club?!

"How about you, Asia? I'm sure you won't mind bathing with your beloved Issei, will you?"

Asia fell silent, her face turning red at the prez's question. She stared down at the floor but soon answered with a slight nod.

Whoa! I had never expected this kind of development! Wh-what was I supposed to do?! I—I was going to have to spend the whole time stooping over so I wouldn't get caught, but it was still doable!

"The only one left is Koneko. What do you think?"

Koneko raised her arms to make an X shape. "...No."

No?! She was daring to deny me this simple pleasure?! I felt paralyzed with shock, but when I stopped to think about it, that *was* a normal response.

"Then I'm afraid we can't. I'm sorry, Issei," Rias said with a mischievous chuckle.

They had all gotten my hopes up, only to cast them down into the abyss. My vision turned dark from the shock. I had been so close to achieving something wonderful... I suppose dreams don't become reality that easily, though. In that case, the next best thing to satisfy myself was taking a—

"...If you peek at us, you'll regret it."

Gah! Koneko struck first! Damn it! Had I come all this way just for it to end like this?!

"Issei, you can bathe with me. I'll wash your back for you."

"Shut up, Kiba! I swear I'll kill you!"

My indignant cries echoed through the cottage.

—○●○—

When I woke up on the second day of our training, I was greeted by pained muscles in every part of my body.

That wasn't particularly surprising, because I'd been training all through the night, too.

"I have a nighttime training regimen planned out for you. We are creatures of the night, after all," the prez had said.

It had been harder work than even my everyday training sessions with her. Rias had given me several times more exercises to do. Even though my demonic strength increased after sundown, that wasn't going to stop me from dropping dead if I couldn't catch a break.

I was already depressed enough, seeing as I had to share a room with Kiba. Every time I heard the girls upstairs break out into laughter, I well and truly regretted having been born a man.

On the morning of the second day, it was time for a study session.

We gathered in the living room so that everyone could impart some general demon knowledge onto Asia and myself.

The lesson was filled with difficult names and associations between different groups and individuals. It was enough to give me a headache.

After filling me with information, Kiba started peppering me with questions.

"What is the name given to our archnemeses, the highest rank of angels who lead the armies of God? And who are their members?"

"Er, the seraphim, right? There's…Michael, Raphael, Gabriel, and… Uriel, wasn't it?"

"Correct."

Phew. I had managed to get it right. The only thing I was 100 percent sure about was that they all ended in the letter *L*, but that hint had been enough.

"Next question. Tell me the names of the Four Great Demon Kings."

"Ah, I know this! I'm going to meet each of them once I've made a name for myself! So I made sure I know who they are! All right, there's Lucifer, Beelzebub, and Asmodeus! And my favorite, the female Demon King, Leviathan!"

"Correct."

"I can't wait to meet Leviathan!"

Naturally. The prez had told me that the highest-ranking female demon was none other than the Demon King Leviathan.

She was said to be especially beautiful! If I was lucky, I'd be able to meet her one day! At least that's what the prez had said! I couldn't wait!

Just how beautiful was she, though? She was a Demon King, so she had to be something special…

I *needed* to meet her!

"In that case, Issei, tell me the names of the leaders of our most despised fallen angels."

Here it was. I *hated* those fallen angels…

Their faction had more leaders than the other two. And their names were particularly hard to remember…

I was confident I remembered the names of the top two, though.

"The main group of fallen angels is called the Grigori, the Watchers of the Children of God. Their Governor is called Azazel, and their Lieutenant Governor is Shemhazai. I know those two. As for the other leaders... There's Armaros...Baraqel...Tamiel...and, er...who again? Bene-something-or-other and, er, C-C-C-Cocaine...?"

"Penemue, Kokabiel, and Sariel. Be sure to remember them. This is basic knowledge. Think of it like knowing the name of the prime minister of Japan and other politicians or the leaders of other countries."

How am I supposed to know all this?! There are too many of them! Isn't two enough?! Just what do the others do anyway?!

Seriously, those fallen angels were a real pain. There was no way I was ever going to like even a single one of them. They were rotten, every single one of them.

Then there was that nonsense about fallen angels watching over the Children of God. In other words, spying on those of us who had Sacred Gears twenty-four-seven. It was fallen angels from that sect who had repeatedly attacked me and who had murdered Asia.

Apparently, they had set up an organization to study Sacred Gears. They would invite seemingly useful holders of any to join their ranks and then try to steal them. Plus, if they thought that someone was too dangerous, they would kill them on the spot. They really were despicable.

They even went so far as to kill those who didn't know they were in possession of a Sacred Gear in the first place, like me.

They were the number one enemy of demonkind, and I swore not to hold back the next time I ran into one of them. Not after what they had done to Asia!

I picked up all kinds of information about angels and fallen angels during the study session. It would probably come in handy one day.

In any event, I had hammered home the important stuff about the relationships between various demons and the other factions.

Next was Asia's turn to deliver a lesson.

"Ahem. I don't mean to sound presumptuous, but I, Asia Argento, will now teach you about exorcists."

Impressive. I wanted to give her a round of applause. Here she was, all grown up and ready to speak in front of everyone.

Her face turned red. Thank you, Asia, for your cute reaction!

"Er, um. Well, there are two kinds of exorcists in the organization that I used to belong to."

"Two kinds?" I repeated in question.

Asia nodded. "The first are like those who you see on television or in movies. A priest might recite a verse from the Holy Book or use holy water to drive a demon from someone's body. They are like the public face of exorcists. It's the private face that is a real threat to demons."

Rias picked up the explanation from there. "You've met one of them before, Issei. Our worst enemies are those exorcists who have received the blessing of God or of the fallen angels. We have been fighting them from the shadows throughout history. They seek to destroy us using the power of light that they receive from angels, and they hone their physical bodies to an otherworldly level."

The image of the young psycho priest I'd fought a while ago flashed in the back of my mind. That white-haired exorcist had been a total lunatic. Not only had he killed demons, he'd also mercilessly eliminated anyone who'd had even the faintest connection to us. He was the kind of person I hoped never to see again.

At that moment, Asia pulled something out from her bag, and the prez picked up a small bottle with the tips of her fingers, as if touching something filthy.

"Now I'll teach you about the properties of holy water and the Holy Book," Asia continued. "I'll start with holy water. It has a horrible effect on demons."

"That's right. Make sure you don't touch it, either, Asia. It will ruin your lovely skin," Rias added.

"Oh, I see… I can't use holy water anymore…" Asia looked legitimately shocked by this. Well, she was a demon now, after all.

"I don't know if you will ever need to, but I'll teach you how to make it later. There's a few ways to do it."

Perhaps because it had been her specialty, Asia looked genuinely happy as she continued her lesson.

She'd become some kind of demon priestess! If I said that to her, though, she was liable to break down in tears. I made sure to restrain myself.

"Next is the Holy Book. I've been reading it every day since I was a child. But now, even reading just a single verse gives me a headache…"

"Well, you *are* a demon."

"That's because you're a demon."

"…A demon."

"My, that's one way to inflict damage."

All at once, the entire group pointed out the same thing to her.

"I can't read it anymore?!" Asia sobbed.

The prez had mentioned earlier that demons would suffer greatly if someone was to read the Bible out loud to us.

I was fortunate enough not to have experienced that yet, but even if I wasn't a demon, I was pretty sure I'd find the book boring.

Despite that, Asia still turned to a page as if she was going to read it! If she went through with it, she could end up killing herself!

"But there's a part I really love… O Lord. Forgive your sinful servant for being unable to— Ah!"

The second Asia started praying, she suffered damage.

God, can't you at least overlook this girl's prayers? I thought.

After completing our morning study session, we moved on to an afternoon of more training.

The endless training I suffered while huddled up in the mountains with the others taught me a great many things.

I had no talent for swordsmanship.

I had no talent for martial arts.

I had no talent for demonic magic.

And above all, I was devastatingly weak.

The more we trained, the more it drove home my inadequacies.

I was going to be useless in the Rating Game.

What's more, there was no chance that I could make a recovery like Asia.

All I was good for now was peeling vegetables. I guess that was a part of my training, too, though.

I was just so weak and useless…

—o●o—

That night, I stared up at the ceiling from my bed in the cottage. A week had passed since we had come to those mountains.

From morning to night, we busied ourselves with training. We tried all kinds of coordination patterns, along with offensive and defensive variations. Again and again, we reviewed them until we knew each one by heart.

I glanced toward Kiba, who was sleeping soundly on the bed beside me. He was incredible. The more we practiced together, the more my respect for him had grown.

No matter what I did, I knew I'd probably never be able to beat him in a sword fight. Long-standing dedication and effort had honed his innate talents to the extreme.

I had neither of those things. How much training would it have taken for my swordsmanship to be a match for his? How many years? How many decades? Even if I dedicated my whole life to it, I didn't see it happening.

I…

Then there were my demonic magic training sessions with Akeno. Asia kept on improving—manipulating flames, water, and lightning, even if none was on a large scale. I, on the other hand, could barely make a mass as small as a single speck.

I... Ahhh, damn it!

I couldn't bear it any longer, and so I sat up in bed. I lifted myself slowly to my feet and headed for the kitchen. As I fixed myself a glass of water and gulped it down...

"Oh? You're awake?" came the prez's voice from the living room. When I looked up, I saw Rias sitting at the table.

"Oh, Prez. Good evening," I said.

"Why are you being so formal? This is good timing, though. Come, let's have a chat."

A weak tea candle was burning on the table. Demons could see in the dark, even without external light, which was how we were able to train in such a desolate place in the dead of night. The candle, then, must have just been for decoration.

I took a seat across from Rias.

She was dressed in a red negligee, her crimson hair tied behind her head, and was wearing glasses.

"Huh? Is your eyesight bad?"

"Oh, these? I just wear them to set the mood. Whenever I have something to think about, putting on a pair of glasses helps me to approach the problem from a different angle. I've been living in the human world for too long." She let out a small chuckle.

Those glasses really looked good on her, though... And that negligee of hers accentuated her body!

There was a pile of papers stacked up on the table. They looked like battle-formation plans... Was she staying up all night working on our strategy?

Rias closed the notebook she was reading from and looked up. "...To be honest with you, reading over all this only gives me so much peace of mind." She let out a tired sigh.

"Why is that?"

"If we were fighting any other high-ranking demon, reading these strategies might be enough. A lot of research has been put into this manual. But that isn't the main issue."

"Huh? Then what's wrong?"

"The problem is Riser himself. Or rather, that our opponent is a phoenix."

Rias pulled out another book and set it on the table in front of me before turning to a specific page. On it was an image of a firebird, its burning wings of flame spread out majestically.

"Long ago, people worshipped the phoenix as a mythical life-controlling creature. Even today, legends remain all throughout the human world. Its tears are said to heal any wound, and drinking its blood can supposedly grant you immortality."

Apparently, there was also another kind of phoenix, distinct from the legendary creature. That was the Phenex clan, a family of demons with the rank of Marquis that was also one of the Seventy-Two Pillars.

"To distinguish the two, humans gave the mythical creature the name of *phoenix*, while labeling the demon family *Phenex*. However, Riser's family possesses practically the same abilities as the legendary bird. In other words, immortality. That is who we must fight."

"Immortality"?! *H-hold on a minute there!*

"That isn't fair! You're saying he's practically invincible?!" I exclaimed.

"Yes, almost. Even if we manage to land an attack on him, he will regenerate and heal himself instantly. Not only that, but his hellfire can incinerate its target, leaving nothing but bones. He has won eight of his ten official Rating Game matches. The two he lost he did so on purpose, out of deference to families that his own House has close ties with. Effectually, he is undefeated. His performance has already made him a candidate for an official title of his own."

I was at a loss for words.

It was clear now what Rias meant when she'd said that we had a problem. It was Riser himself! She was trying to find a way to defeat that bastard!

"I had a sense of foreboding right from the moment Riser was selected as my fiancé. My father and the others must have been planning for this from the very beginning. They chose Riser so that I would have no choice but to get married. Even if I was resistant to the idea, they knew that if it came down to deciding the matter through a match, I wouldn't stand a chance of winning. They cornered me. In chess terminology, they played a swindle."

No matter how strong Rias was, her parents must have known that she wouldn't be able to beat someone who was immortal. Talk about unfair! No one would've stood a chance against someone like Riser!

"When the Rating Game became popular in demon society, it was the House of Phenex who benefited the most. Before that advent, demons didn't really fight among one another very often. But in the Rating Game, where the King participates along with their servants, the advantage held by the members of the Phenex family is undeniable. Which is why their House is at the top of the highest class in the official rankings. Immortality. Perhaps it was only through seeing how they performed at the game that other demons realized how terrifying that power truly is."

If Riser and the other members of his clan were immortal, then they would automatically be revived no matter how many times they were defeated. Normal demons didn't have unlimited power. So even if they were stronger than someone like Riser, they would eventually succumb to exhaustion and defeat. If you asked me, though, I thought that kind of overwhelming advantage was pretty cowardly!

That still didn't change the fact that we were going to face a truly fearsome opponent.

Even if we managed to take down his army of beautiful servants, that wouldn't mean anything if we couldn't defeat him, too. Was it even possible? It really seemed like this whole arrangement had been rigged from the beginning.

Perhaps my uncertainty was writ large on my face, as Rias let out a chuckle. "But it isn't like we won't be able to find some way to win."

"Seriously?!"

"Indeed. There are two options. We can crush him with overwhelming force, or we can break his spirit by knocking him down over and over. To try the first method would require a godlike level of power. The second option would require us to conserve our energy and stamina until we can crush his will to fight. I'm certain each defeat will take a toll on him. Even if his body is immortal and can be continuously restored to fighting form, his mind isn't. Each loss will tire him out. And if we can do that, then victory will be within our grasp. That said, if we *did* have a godlike power at our disposal, it *would* be a lot easier to go with the first option..."

To me, it seemed clear that both of Rias's strategies were impossible without considerable effort. Could we really pull something like that off in our first match? I suppose there was little other choice.

Basically, we would have to keep going until Riser lost the will to fight and asked to call off the match. Considering that, I remembered that there was something I'd wanted to ask for a while now.

"Prez."

"Yes?"

"Why do you hate him so much...? I mean, why are you so set against marrying him?"

At this question, Rias let out a tired exhale.

Riser was undeniably a womanizer and a lowlife, but given Rias's family situation, it didn't sound like she could afford to turn him down.

"...Because I'm a Gremory."

"Huh? W-well, that's true..."

"No, it isn't just a word. I belong to the House of Gremory, and that name will follow me no matter where I go."

Ah, so that's it.

"You don't like your name?"

"I'm proud to be a Gremory. But it's also destroying me as an individual. Everyone sees me only as Rias Gremory—never simply as Rias.

That's why I enjoy the human world so much. No one knows anything about the demonic House of Gremory here. People see me as me. I love this place. I could never feel the things I do here if I was to confine myself to demon society. I can only live a life of fulfilment, as an individual, here." There was a distant look to Rias's eyes as she spoke, and sadness fell over her.

What she was describing was something I had never experienced myself. I was simply Issei Hyoudou, and that name didn't instill any particular depth of feeling in me. I was just me, the son of my father and mother.

No matter where I went, people recognized me as an individual. But Rias's whole life had been spent carrying the weight of the name of Gremory on her back. And that would continue to be the case for her.

"I want to be loved by someone who sees me not as a Gremory but as Rias. That's my selfish dream... Unfortunately, to Riser, I'm always Rias Gremory. That's who he loves. I can't stand that. My family pride is still important to me, though. It might sound rather contradictory, but I want to cherish this small dream of mine..."

So the prez wanted to be loved by a man not as Rias Gremory but simply as Rias... It was a very maidenly sentiment. No doubt the reason why she felt so conflicted was because of her family's current predicament.

I didn't know much about the feelings of young women or about the complexities of demon society, so I wasn't entirely sure what was best to say, and yet...

"I like you, Prez, just as yourself," I said.

Rias's eyes widened slightly.

"I'm not very knowledgeable when it comes to the House of Gremory or to the demon world, but to me, you're just you... I'm not really good at all this complicated stuff, but as far as I'm concerned, the everyday Rias is the best!" It was all I could do to just blurt out everything that came to mind and give the prez a broad smile.

Ha. I really wasn't very good at saying anything cool or romantic.

Perhaps it'd only been my imagination, but for a moment, I could've sworn I saw Rias's cheeks turn red.

"P-Prez? D-did I say something strange?" I asked uncertainly.

She shook her head. "I-it's nothing!" she responded, flustered.

I wasn't sure what that had been about, but there were more important things to consider at the moment.

"Still, it's going to be a challenge, facing off against someone like that in your first match. Even for a genius like you."

"I don't like that word, *'genius,'*" Rias answered, her face still red.

"Why not?"

"…The Romans used that word to describe a divine nature in every living thing. Christians associate it with the soul. And the Japanese equivalent, *tensai*, means a talent bestowed from Heaven. That's why I don't like it. It makes it sound like a gift from God. My talents are the fruition of the hard work of generations of Gremorys. I've inherited them as a demon. God would never grant them to me, and I've never thought of them in that way. My powers belong to my House. That's why I won't lose. I will fight, and I will win. I have to." By the end, she sounded almost as if she was trying to convince herself.

Rias was so incredible and strong. Compared to her, I…

"Prez, I-I'm sorry. I've been useless…since the moment we came here," I murmured weakly.

A look of concern arose on Rias's face. "Issei?"

"I know I've gotten stronger from training with everyone, but more than that…I can feel just how far I still have to go to catch up. Practicing swordsmanship with Kiba only reminds me just how skilled he is, and all I can think of is that I'll never be a great swordsman like him… When I practice using my powers with Akeno, I can *feel* how talented she is. Plus, I keep watching Asia get better and better, while I still can't do anything… I tried to act like everything would be fine so long as I had the Boosted Gear, but I know it isn't…"

Before I knew it, tears were running down my cheeks.

I was beyond frustrated. The more I felt, the more I understood just how mediocre I was.

I had no talent for combat.

I knew that now.

"I know I'm the weakest... I know I'm the most useless... An all-powerful Sacred Gear means nothing so long as I'm the one using it. That's why Riser made a fool of me. *'A worthless treasure. Pearls before swine.'* He was right."

There I was, bawling my eyes out in front of the prez. I must have looked pathetic, weeping uncontrollable tears of frustration. Even my nose was dripping.

Rias rose to her feet and came to sit next to me.

—!

She took me in her arms, hugging me gently. She patted me on the head again and again.

"You need confidence, don't you? That's okay; I'll give it to you. But you need to let your body and mind rest. I'll stay with you until you can drift off to sleep."

At the time, I didn't recognize exactly what she meant, but I could feel her warmth healing my soul.

That was enough.

"Use your Boosted Gear, Issei!" Rias called out to me at the start of my next training session the following morning.

For the first time since we'd come to these mountains, she was giving me permission to use my Sacred Gear... But what did she expect me to do with it?

"Let's have you face off against Yuuto."

"Understood." At the prez's urging, Kiba came forward to stand across from me.

Hold on. Is she telling me to fight him?!

"Issei, let's say you activated your Sacred Gear before we started this mock battle. We can begin…say, two minutes after you call it."

"R-right."

As instructed, I made the Boosted Gear appear over my left arm.

"Boost!" I called out, and…

"Boost!" sounded the Sacred Gear in return.

I could feel the energy flowing through my body, doubling my latent power.

Ten seconds passed.

"Boost!"

Again came another compound doubling of my abilities. Power surged from the Sacred Gear through my body.

Increasing my power this way was all well and good, but there were a few things that I had to be careful of while using the Boosted Gear. While I'd initially assumed that there was no limit to how far my ability could've been increased, that wasn't the case. One time I'd tried activating it just to see how far it would go, but I'd ended up fainting after only a few minutes.

The reason was simple enough. My body couldn't handle all that extra power.

The prez had outlined a pretty simple way for me to understand. "If you had a truck, and if you loaded it far beyond its normal capacity, what would happen? It wouldn't be able to move, would it? The same thing applies here."

Basically, if you kept loading too many things onto a vehicle, the added weight would keep making it slower and slower, until eventually it was unable to move at all.

In other words, too much power put a heavy strain on my body. That was why I had fainted. I simply couldn't withstand that much extra energy.

At the time, when the gemstone embedded in the back of the gauntlet had shouted out the word *"Burst!"* my whole body had grown heavy, and everything seemed to just stop.

Even if the Boosted Gear itself had virtually unlimited power, I, its user, didn't. That was the ultimate weakness of this Sacred Gear. Or rather, that was *my* weakness. It wasn't the Sacred Gear's fault.

After twelve power-ups, Rias ordered me not to increase my power any further.

"All right! Let's go, Boosted Gear!" I said.

"Explosion!"

That sound acted as a stopper and meant that my Sacred Gear understood that I had powered up enough.

Once I reached a certain level, I could maintain that state and fight for a while. The length of time essentially depended on how I spent that extra energy. The more I moved or attacked, the shorter I had. My stamina level also played a role. Being tired meant less time, too. That was why the best way to use the Boosted Gear was to avoid taking damage.

I was well rested and uninjured that morning, meaning that was the best time to use it.

Fighting while the Sacred Gear was still powering up my abilities was doable, but it made my power more unstable compared to when I put a stop to the continued doubling. What's more, making a mistake risked resetting everything back to zero. As such, it was safer to fight only after pausing the process.

As far as I knew, the best thing to do was to evade all oncoming attacks and hide while I was charging up.

Having let my Boosted Gear do its thing for a full two minutes, my power level had reached an abnormally high state.

"I want you to stay like that, Issei, and fight Yuuto as you are now. Yuuto, I'll leave Issei to you."

"Yes, President," Kiba responded, readying himself and pointing his wooden practice sword in my direction.

"Issei, do you want to use a sword? Or would you prefer to fight barehanded?" Rias asked me.

Hmm, I wondered. Even if I did try to use a sword, I still wasn't very skilled at wielding one...

"I'll fight barehanded!" I answered.

"Very well. In that case, please begin."

I adopted a fighting posture. Well, a beginner's fighting posture.

Whoom.

All of a sudden, Kiba completely disappeared! Uh-oh! One of a Knight's main attributes was their agility! Kiba possessed an almost godlike speed! If I lost sight of him, he wouldn't have any difficulty—

Clang!

Kiba's attack came rushing toward me, but I managed to parry it with my arm. All right! I could do this!

"—!" A look of surprise flashed across his face.

An opening! I rushed toward it, unleashing a punch.

Flash!

Before my fist could reach its target, Kiba disappeared once more, leaving me to strike nothing but empty air. He'd dodged it!

Where did he go? I scanned my surroundings, but he wasn't there! If he wasn't to my left or right, and if he wasn't in front, then he could've only been behind me, right?

Spinning around in expectation, I was surprised to see he wasn't there, either.

Is he above me?! I looked upward, only to find him hurtling down with his wooden blade.

Thump!

There was a dull *thud*. Ugh! Kiba had struck me right on the head. Damn it, that hurt!

"Ouch..."

With no time to see how badly I'd been injured, I unleashing a kick where Kiba had landed.

Whoosh!

He vanished again! Damn him! I couldn't hit him at all! Were these Knights simply too fast for me to land an attack?!

"Issei! Use your powers! Gather them all together and unleash them in the first image that comes to mind!" the prez instructed.

Attack with my powers? Me? Where? I had no idea where Kiba was, but there was little else to do but try at that point.

I focused the energy flowing through me into the palm of my hand until I had a mass no larger than a grain of rice. Nothing had changed, even after practicing.

Aiming the little blip of light at Kiba, I tried to fire it forward—only to be left shocked by what happened next.

Boooooooooom!

It was huge! That pinprick of energy had swelled into something enormous!

It was like a gigantic boulder! Was this the result of using the Boosted Gear?!

That enormous mass of power sped toward Kiba at incredible speed. *Swoosh.*

He still dodged it easily, though. That wasn't particularly surprising. No matter how impressive my attack was, it didn't mean a thing if it couldn't find its mark. At least, that's what I thought at the time. But what happened next quickly convinced me otherwise.

Having missed its target, that huge sphere of energy flew off into the distance, only to crash into the next mountain over.

Booooooooooooooooooooom!

The whole mountainside exploded with a thunderous roar!

Huh?! What?! You're kidding me, right?!

A single blast of my accumulated power had been enough to blow away the entire mountainside. When the dust settled, there was a gaping hole gouged in the side of it, reshaping the scenery entirely.

...Huh? Seriously? Did I actually just destroy a mountain?!

Such an unexpected turn of events had left me completely speechless.

"Reset!" echoed the voice from my gauntlet, and all at once, the power raging through my body left me.

I had run out of time.

Suddenly, I was feeling strangely empty. I must have exhausted my powers.

"That's enough," Rias declared, calling off the practice duel.

Kiba lowered his sword, and I slumped down to the ground.

The mountain was gone.

My heart raced at the shock of it all. *Did I really just do that?* That an attack like that had really come from my own two hands seemed like a bit too much to grasp.

"Good work, you two. Now, I want to hear your thoughts. Yuuto, how was Issei?" Rias asked.

"Okay," Kiba responded. "To tell you the truth, that was astonishing. I'd expected my first attack to end the battle."

Huh? Does he mean the one I parried right at the beginning?

"But I couldn't break through Issei's guard, and not for lack of trying, either. I had also hoped to knock him off his feet with that blow from above, but that proved ineffective as well." Kiba let out a charming laugh before raising his wooden practice sword for everyone to see.

It was cracked right down the middle.

"Even though I'd strengthened my blade with my powers, Issei's body was too sturdy. If we'd kept on going, I would've broken my weapon and been unable to launch any further attacks."

"Thank you, Yuuto," Rias said. "Do you understand now, Issei?"

I wondered if this was what the prez had meant the previous night when she'd said that she would give me confidence.

"Issei, you told me that you thought you were the weakest of my servants and that you had no talent, didn't you?" Rias asked.

"Y-yeah…"

"That was only half-correct. Without your Boosted Gear, you *are* weak. But when you activate it, you climb to a whole new level." Rias motioned toward the destroyed mountain in the distance. "That final attack was on the level of a high-class demon. Something like that would've defeated almost any opponent."

Seriously?! I couldn't really imagine many people surviving a blow like that, but still…

"Thanks to the basic training, your body is now a vessel capable of accumulating an enormous amount of energy. Already, that power is quite the formidable force. Didn't I tell you? Discipline yourself, master the essentials, and you will be more powerful than anyone. The more you advance your basic stats, the more your abilities will grow with exponential returns. Even increasing them from level one to level two will make an enormous difference."

—! *Am I really that amazing?* I still could hardly believe it.

Rias gave me an assuring expression. "You are essential to the upcoming match. Your attack power, Issei, will decide the outcome of the battle. If you were fighting alone, the amount of time it would take to charge your skills would leave you terribly vulnerable, but this is a team game. You have allies who will defend you. Believe in us. Do that, and we'll all be stronger for it. We'll win!"

...Stronger... Me?

"Let's show them who we really are!" Rias raised her voice in a rallying cry. "We won't let them make fools of us anymore. It doesn't matter if our opponent is a phoenix; we'll show them the strength of Rias Gremory and her Familia!"

"Yeah!" everyone cried out in unison.

That's right, I realized. I wasn't alone. The prez and the others all stood with me!

With renewed determination, I promised myself I'd get stronger. I was going to improve and stand shoulder to shoulder with my friends and allies!

We were going to defeat Riser Phenex!

Amid our united resolve and sense of camaraderie, the last few days of training passed without issue.

Then came the day of the decisive showdown.

Life.4
The Showdown Begins!

The day of the decisive showdown had arrived.

"All right!" I said, trying to fire myself up in my room.

It was ten o'clock at night. The battle was due to begin in two hours, at exactly midnight.

We'd all been told to take the day off from demon work, heading straight home after school. The idea was to be as refreshed and rested as possible when the time came for the Rating Game.

Our plan was to meet in the clubroom thirty minutes before the beginning of the match. That gave me just over one hour. Still, my bedroom was the place where I could most relax, so I wanted to stay there for as long as I could.

If I was to go to the clubroom ahead of time, I wouldn't be able to stop myself from fretting. Even as I tried to rest in my room, I was more nervous than I'd been during my high school entrance exams...

I was wearing my school uniform; I'd thought that the most appropriate. When I'd asked the prez whether we should have a sort of team combat uniform, she'd brushed my question aside with a smile: "If my Familia has a uniform, it has to be that of Kuou Academy. We are the Occult Research Club, after all."

Thus, my school uniform had become my battle uniform. That said,

I guess I could have gone with a martial-arts outfit or something if I'd wanted to...

There was a mountain of banana peels next to me. I had already finished eating the fruit and was close to perfecting my special technique that I had been working on since the first day of our training camp.

I can do this! This is my new ultimate technique!

Knock-knock, came a sound from my door. It had to have been Asia.

"Issei, can I come in?" she asked.

"Ah, sure."

When she entered my room, I was completely taken aback after seeing her outfit.

It was a nun's outfit. Of course, she wasn't carrying any rosaries, nor was she wearing a veil over her head.

"Asia, what are you...?"

"I—I know. When I asked the president, she told me to wear whatever I felt most comfortable in. I didn't really know what to choose, but then I thought that this would be easiest to move around in... I may not be a servant of the Lord anymore, but I haven't renounced my faith. Even if I am a demon now..."

It seemed Asia had put a lot of thought into it.

There was no small amount of courage involved in dressing like a nun for a battle between demons, but if that was what she had decided, then I wasn't about to voice any complaint. I was sure Rias would brush it off with a laugh.

"I see. I suppose you do look most natural in that. Your school uniform suits you, too, you know, but seeing as this is what you were wearing when we first met, I guess it's kind of how I always imagine you. It looks good on you."

"Thank you." Asia's face beamed with heartfelt joy at my compliment. "U-um, Issei...," she said, suddenly fidgeting. "Can I sit next to you?"

"A-ah, sure."

She sat herself down next to me on my bed and then took my arm, hugging it tight.

"Wh-what's wrong?" I asked, worried. I could feel her trembling as she gripped my arm.

"...When I think about the match, I can't stop shaking. I'm scared. But I'll be all right, so long as you're there with me."

"Asia..."

"Hee-hee. Yep, I'm not scared when I'm with you, Issei... Can we stay like this until it's time to go?"

"Sure."

"...Can we stay like this forever?"

"Yep, forever."

"...Thank goodness."

I took her trembling hands in my own. We passed a few moments in blissful silence.

When the time came for us to leave, I was totally relaxed. Asia had stopped shaking, too.

—o●o—

It must have been around 11:40 at night. The other members of Rias's Familia and I had gathered in the clubroom in the old school building. Each one of us was trying to pass the time in our own way. Everyone except Asia was wearing their school uniform, albeit with a few modifications.

Kiba's hands and wrists were protected by padded coverings, and his lower legs were protected by some kind of armor-like shin guards. He had left his sword leaning by the wall.

Koneko was sitting in her chair reading a book. Her hands were garbed in a pair of open-finger gloves, the kind that martial artists used. It was an eerily serious look for such a childlike figure.

Akeno and the prez were sitting on the sofa, elegantly sipping their cups of tea. As was to be expected of the Two Great Ladies, they were composed to the last.

Asia and I were sitting in our seats, quietly idling away the remaining time.

Ten minutes before the match was due to begin, the magic circle in the center of the room lit up, and Grayfia made her entrance.

"Have you completed your preparations? The match will begin in ten minutes," she said.

We each rose to our feet, and Grayfia began her explanation. "When it is time, you will all be transported to the arena through your magic circle. The match will take place in a neutral alternative space, a dimension created and set aside solely for this battle. Feel free to fight to your full potential. We will discard the battlefield when we are finished, so don't worry about causing any damage."

Ah. That makes sense, I thought. An artificial battlefield. I hadn't known that demons were able to create spaces like this.

I understood the need for something like that, though. If we were to fight in either the human realm or the demon world, there was no telling how much damage we could end up causing. A place that could be destroyed without consequence was the perfect location.

Putting that aside for a moment, there was still something I wasn't entirely sure about.

"Um, Prez?"

"Yes?"

"You said you had another Bishop, right? Is that person coming?"

When Rias had resurrected Asia as a demon, she'd said that she already had one other Bishop.

She'd told me that person was off somewhere taking care of a special job for her. This situation definitely felt serious enough to warrant them joining us, though.

No sooner had I asked the question, however, than everyone's faces, excepting Asia's and my own, turned stiff. The atmosphere had undergone a complete shift. The mood in the room had grown incredibly heavy. For a short while, no one said a word.

"I'm afraid my other Bishop isn't able to join us," Rias answered, averting her gaze. "We'll have to talk about that sometime soon."

Whatever the reason could've been, it was clearly a difficult topic for the prez. I thought it best not to pry any further. Still, I had to wonder what could've been so important that the other Bishop wasn't showing up for such an important match. Rias's evasive response just left me with more questions.

It was Grayfia who broke the sullen atmosphere. "Representatives from both noble Houses will be following this Rating Game by way of live broadcast."

Seriously? They're gonna be watching the whole thing? How nice for those high-class demon parents. Still, if Rias's folks were looking on, then I had to be careful with how I presented myself.

"In addition, His Lordship the Demon King Lucifer will be observing. Do keep that in mind."

"The Demon King"?! Whoa, now I was really on edge! To think that one of the guys at the top was taking an interest in us!

Rias, however, looked shocked. "My brother...? I see, so he'll be there, too..."

Had I misheard? Surely Rias hadn't just said...

I raised my hand with a new question. "Um, Prez, did you just call the Demon King your brother...? Did I mishear?"

"You heard her correctly. The president's brother is one of the four Demon Kings." It was Kiba who answered.

What...?

"A-a Demon King?! Y-your brother is a Demon King?!"

"Yes," Rias answered plainly.

Is she serious?! Hold on a second, I thought. *Rias belongs to the House of Gremory. None of the Demon Kings has that name, though...*

Lucifer, Beelzebub, Leviathan, Asmodeus. None of them sounded anything like Gremory!

"Are you wondering why the president's family name is different from those of the Demon Kings?"

As much as I hated to admit it, Kiba had guessed exactly what I was thinking.

"Yeah." I nodded with reluctance.

"The original Demon Kings perished in the Great War. Nonetheless, demon society is nothing without its leadership. As such—"

Kiba went on to explain that the surviving demons decided to grant the names of the Demon Kings to their most powerful members. For that reason, the current Four Great Demon Kings had inherited their ultimate titles from their predecessors, the first generation.

That made sense. Since that was the case, names like Lucifer and Beelzebub were more like titles.

"To tell the truth, among the forces of God, the fallen angels, and us demons, we're currently the least powerful faction. The situation is rather precarious, but as our current kings are just as formidable as their forebears, we've been able to endure."

Apparently, demon society was hanging on by a thread.

It certainly came as a shock to learn that the famous demons written about in books that you might find in a library were already dead.

"In that case, you're saying that the prez's brother was chosen to be one of those ultimate high-class demons?" I asked.

Kiba nodded. "Sirzechs Lucifer, the Crimson Satan. He's both the president's elder brother and the most powerful demon alive."

Sirzechs Lucifer.

Not Gremory but Lucifer. It sounded like he wasn't part of her family anymore.

"...So that's why the prez needs to inherit the House of Gremory?"

If her elder brother had become a Demon King, then it sounded like she had no choice in the matter. Her brother had to hold the weight of all of demon society on his shoulders. That was incredible. His relation to Rias seemed that much more unbelievable...

"It's almost time. Everyone, please step into the magic circle."

At Grayfia's request, we all gathered in the center of the room.

"Once you have been transported to the arena, you won't be able to return until the completion of the match," she explained.

No coming back until it's over, huh?

The insignia in the magic circle shifted into an unfamiliar pattern before erupting with light. It hadn't been the pattern of the Phenex family, either. Perhaps it'd been a custom design made especially for the Rating Game?

Those were my last thoughts before we were all swallowed by light and warped to our destination.

—○●○—

I opened my eyes.

...*Huh?* I tilted my head to the side in bewilderment at what I saw. Anybody would have. I mean, we were still in the clubroom.

Had the magic circle failed? Apart from Asia and myself, no one else seemed the least bit surprised.

Grayfia was conspicuously missing, however. Was she the only one who'd successfully made the jump?

But at that moment—

"Welcome, everyone. I, Grayfia, servant to the House of Gremory, will act as Arbiter for today's Rating Game between the House of Gremory and the House of Phenex."

It sounded like a school announcement, but it was Grayfia's voice.

"In the name of His Lordship Sirzechs Lucifer, I will ensure the fairness and impartiality of today's proceedings. Based on Lady Rias and Lord Riser's mutual wishes, the battlefield will be a replica of the school that Lady Rias attends in the human world, Kuou Academy."

What?! Th-then this is all a fake? But it looks identical! Even the decorations and wear and tear on the walls are exactly the same! My jaw dropped.

Then I noticed that the sky outside the window was pure white. We'd all met in the clubroom just before midnight, so that didn't make any sense. Did this replica exist in some pale, empty dimension, then?

I had to wonder just how powerful these demons were if they were able to make an entirely new alternate dimension for the sake of one battle.

"Both teams have been transported to an area that will serve as their respective home bases. Lady Rias, your home base will be the clubroom of the Occult Research Club in the old school building. Lord Riser, yours will be located in the student council room in the new school building. All Pawns, please proceed to the immediate vicinity of the opposing team's home base when using a Promotion."

That was me! Basically, what this meant was that I couldn't Promote unless I made my way to Riser's camp. Given my attributes as a Pawn, finding a way to pull off a Promotion was going to be essential if we were to aim for victory.

Just like in the game of chess, a Promotion was a special move that a Pawn could use when reaching a set position deep behind the opposing team's lines. It allowed them to transform into any piece other than a King.

Basically, I had to make sure I could enter the other team's home base. The student council room… It was on the top floor of the school building. That was my goal!

By the same logic, Riser's Pawns would be Promoted if they made their way to where I was. Plus, unlike our team, he had eight of them. Each one could end up transforming into a Queen!

Given that the Queen was the most powerful piece, we would be in serious trouble if that happened.

From what I gathered, a common strategy during these matches was for each team to send out its Pawns first to reduce the number of pieces on the battlefield. Did that mean that I had to take down eight beautiful Pawn ladies all by myself? Things were certainly shaping up to be pretty tough for me.

"Everyone, please put these communication devices in your ears," Akeno said, handing out some kind of earphone-like transceiver to each of us.

I did as instructed, and the prez's voice sounded in my ear. "This is how we will coordinate on the battlefield."

Being able to receive instructions remotely? This sounded like it was going to be an extremely valuable item. I had to make sure I didn't break it.

"It's time. The match will continue until there is a victor or until dawn in the human world. Let the game begin."

Ding-dong-dang-dong.

The school bell echoed across the campus. I guess that was the signal.

So it was that the curtain rose on our Rating Game!

—○●○—

"First things first, we need to eliminate Riser's Pawns. We'll be in trouble if all eight of them can Promote into Queens," Rias said from her seat on the sofa. She was surprisingly calm.

Akeno began to prepare some tea.

Uh, aren't we in the middle of a match...? I thought.

"Y-you're pretty calm about this, Prez..."

"The match has only just begun, Issei. A Rating Game isn't something you complete in a short period of time. Naturally, there are cases where one side will attempt to rush the other, but in general, these are long affairs. Just like in the real game of chess."

I had imagined that we would end up fighting a huge battle scene like you see in the movies... Some kind of chaotic ultimate showdown.

"In a Rating Game, you have to use the battlefield to the fullest. In most cases, each team will have its base situated in a fort, a castle, or a tower. Areas such as forests, rivers, and lakes are usually located between the two bases, and these are typically where individual battles are fought. In this case, the battlefield is our school. Yuuto?"

"Right away." At Rias's prompting, Kiba unfolded a large map on the table. It was a layout of the campus and its buildings.

Lines crisscrossed the paper, dividing it into a large grid marked with numbers and letters.

Immediately, I recognized that it was laid out like a checkerboard.

Rias circled the old school building and the new school building with a red pen. Those were the locations of both bases.

"There is a forest near our base. Think of this as being within our territory. On the other hand, the new school building is within Riser's territory. The moment you step inside, you will have entered his domain. The new school building has a complete view of the schoolyard, so it will be dangerous for us to pass through it."

Rias was right. You could make out almost the entire grounds from the windows of the new school building. Now that the match had begun, we couldn't use the magic circle to teleport across the battlefield. In other words, there were no shortcuts.

We would have to approach on foot. Using our wings to fly wasn't out of the question but it would be very conspicuous. Then there was the matter of me still being unable to fly.

"What if we crossed the athletic track and tried sneaking in through the back?" I asked.

Rias gave me a forced smile. "That's the most obvious entry point, and Riser will know it… He will no doubt have dispatched at least one of his pieces near the athletic clubhouse, probably a Rook or a Knight. No, it's a wide-open space, so he'll want mobility. Most likely, he's positioning a Knight and three Pawns there for a total of four pieces. That will give him complete control over the area."

"President, perhaps we should occupy the gymnasium by the old school building?" Kiba suggested. "That will give us a shorter route to the new school building. It's adjacent to both the old and the new school buildings, so it will limit their movements."

Rias nodded. "Yes, I thought so, too. We should take the gymnasium first… Given the location, our opponent may have positioned a Rook there. It will be close quarters, so strength will be more important than a Knight's agility."

Whoa… All this strategizing was going over my head! I would be fine if I only worried about my instructions, though! I had to do my best not to create any problems.

"...Yuuto, Koneko. I want you two to lay traps in the forest. Take another map with you, and be sure to mark where you set your snares. I will give everyone copies when you're finished."

"Yes."

"...Understood."

Kiba and Koneko left at once, taking a map and some odd-looking equipment with them.

"Everyone else, I want you to remain here on standby until they are finished. Ah, Akeno?"

"Yes?"

"Once Yuuto and Koneko return, can you cast a mist and some illusions over the forest and sky? Ones that will only affect members of Riser's Familia, of course. Things are sure to heat up once we reach the middle phase, so I'll leave that to you, Akeno."

"Very good, President." Akeno nodded.

With that, our operations had begun. Neither I nor Asia had received any instructions, though.

"U-uh, Prez? What do you want me to do?" I hated the idea of standing by and doing nothing. I wanted a task, too!

"Indeed. You're my Pawn, Issei, which means that you need to be Promoted," Rias replied.

"Right!" I responded eagerly.

The prez beckoned to me.

Huh? What does she want me to do? I wondered.

"Sit here," she instructed.

No sooner had I taken my seat than she pointed at her lap. "Lay down here."

—! S-seriously?! The legendary lap pillow?!

Was it really okay to just lay my head down on her immaculate white legs?

"Th-thank you!" I beamed, instinctively bowing my head in appreciation.

Gulp... I swallowed, and little by little, I lowered myself toward her thighs.

Plop.

A soft sensation pressed against my cheek.

Whoa! They're so soft, Prez! I was touching her thighs! This level of physical contact was lethal for a guy my age! I wanted to rub my face against her skin, but I restrained myself.

"Oh..." Before I knew it, tears were forming in my eyes.

A lap pillow. Out of the hundreds of things I wanted to do with a girl, this had to rank among my top ten. That it had at last become a reality was almost too overwhelming.

The tears kept rolling down my face. *What am I doing?* I thought. *Shouldn't I be focusing on the match?*

Still, for a perverted high schooler like me who had never been popular with girls, this was a dream come true. I offered a silent word of thanks to my mom and dad for having brought me into the world.

Seeing my reaction, Rias sighed. "Are you crying?"

"*Sniff,* I'm just so moved that you let me lay my head on your lap. I can't stop. I'll never forget this feeling. I'm so happy to be alive."

"You do overreact sometimes. If a lap pillow is enough to make you feel that way, then I'll let you do it again."

What?! Y-you're kidding me! Really?! Why is she being so nice?! It wasn't important to me anyway. All that mattered was that Rias had given me the okay to do it again!

There was no way I wasn't going to take her up on that. Man, my school life sure had gotten pretty great recently. I was moving further and further past Matsuda and Motohama. I did feel a little sorry for them, though. The best I could do for my friends was to hope that they, too, would come to know this pleasure one day.

Huh?! That's when I noticed that Asia was staring at me with teary

eyes of her own! Perhaps it was only my imagination, but it looked like she was pouting.

Is she angry? Why? I didn't quite understand, but it definitely appeared that way.

Rias rested her hand on my head. "…This will release a small part of the seal that I placed on you."

"Huh? A seal?" I asked uncertainly, but at that moment, something inside me swelled.

Thud!

Energy welled up from deep in my body, but I had no idea why. It was an incredible feeling but one wholly different from when I used the Boosted Gear. The power from my Sacred Gear flowed into me from somewhere externally. This new strength was instead rising up from inside me and melting comfortably through my flesh.

The question was, where had it come from?

Likely seeing the bewilderment on my face, Rias leaned into my ear. "Don't you remember? When I resurrected you, I used all eight of my Pawn pieces."

"Yeah…"

"At that time, you were still too underdeveloped as a demon, so I limited the total capacity of your abilities as a Pawn. No normal human would've been able to withstand the full force of eight Pawn pieces so soon after being resurrected. To put this simply, your total strength is second only to Akeno's. However, until you learn to handle that power, you'll be at risk of it breaking you. As such, I locked it away in stages with these seals. I've just released the first of them."

If she had released it, then did that mean this force surging through me was my own innate strength?

"Your training was intended to increase your compatibility not only with the Boosted Gear but also with your own abilities. Admittedly, you still have a way to go, though."

So there *had* been a point to all those grueling exercises! I was so happy that I'd been able to overcome so many near-death experiences!

Rias stroked my head.

It sure was wonderful having a beautiful lady pet my hair.

I could've sworn I saw Asia's eyes narrow even further, however.

"Listen here, Issei. Even if your opponent is a girl, you must still defeat her. You mustn't hold back. They won't show you any mercy."

"R-right!"

"Good boy. When you perform your Promotion, make sure you become a Queen. Queens are the strongest pieces on the field. If you do that, it will turn the match in our favor."

"It feels a bit weird for a guy to become a Queen, though…"

Rias chuckled at my comment. "It's only a name. Don't think too deeply about it. We have fewer members than Riser, which puts us at a disadvantage. You have to be prepared to take on other roles. Losing even one of our members is sure to make this fight much more difficult."

It sounded like Rias had put a lot of thought into each of our roles and was looking for a way to best utilize us all on the field. For a moment, I wondered if charging my powers and then releasing a burst of energy at the new school building would finish the match quickly. Then I realized it probably wouldn't be that easy. Riser definitely would've anticipated a move like that and had probably already prepared countermeasures.

There was a limit to how many moves I could make while powered up, and I wasn't particularly skilled at using my demonic powers, so I couldn't afford to waste them. If I was going to attack, it would be safer to do so, and not to mention more effective, after I'd Promoted myself to a Queen.

Yep, I would just have to trust in Rias and the others to help me get to where I needed to go!

"Prez! I'm going to help you win this!" I was serious. Those words came from the bottom of my heart.

Upon hearing my oath, Rias broke into a gentle smile. "I look forward to it, my cute little Issei."

I was definitely going to help the prez win! There was no way I was about to let her marry someone like Riser!

Rias's wonderful legs were mine to enjoy right up until Kiba and Koneko returned.

Thanks to that, I was bursting with energy!

"All right!" I declared with mighty determination as I stood outside the entrance to the old school building.

Koneko was standing beside me. She was my partner for the next stage of our strategy.

"Very well. Issei, Koneko. Once you enter the building, you won't be able to avoid a battle. Stick to the plan. The gymnasium will be crucial," Rias said, seeing us off at the entrance.

Koneko nodded.

"Don't worry about us," I added.

Our destination was the school gym. There was sure to be a battle there, and Koneko and I were going to win it. Losing wasn't an option. I wasn't about to get knocked out of the Rating Game without first scoring a Promotion!

"I'll start things on my end as well." Kiba, holding his sword against his waist, was ready, too.

"Yuuto, please be sure to follow my instructions," Rias cautioned.

"Understood."

"Asia, you will stay here with me for now. However, once Issei and Koneko give the signal, we'll move out. We can't afford to lose you. Without our healer, we will have no chance."

"O-okay!" Asia replied loudly in spite of her obvious trepidation.

Her healing ability was our lifeline. Thanks to her, we could afford to take a few risks in our overall approach.

Protecting both Asia and our King was necessary for us to come out of this on top.

"Akeno, I'll trust you to move when the time is right."

"Yes, President."

Akeno was Rias's strongest servant. According to Rias, a large portion of this mission's success hinged on her performance. We were all counting on those insidious demonic powers hidden behind that warm smile of hers!

Having looked over everyone one last time, Rias stepped forward. "Very well, my cute servants. I hope you're all ready. There's no turning back now. Our enemy is Riser Phenex, the prodigy of the immortal House of Phenex. Let's crush him!"

"*Yeah!*" we all cried out in unison before taking off.

Kiba, Koneko, and I dashed from the old school building.

"Issei! Everyone! Good luck!" Asia called out in encouragement. She was waving to us from the entrance.

All right, you can't turn back now, Issei Hyoudou! Be ready to break through!

We approached the gymnasium. Partway there, Kiba branched off in another direction, as per the plan.

"I'll see you up ahead!" he called out.

"Wait for us there!" I shouted in reply.

With that, we split up. He had his job to do, and I had mine!

Together with Koneko, I made my way toward the gymnasium.

The main entrance was connected to the new school building, making it unlikely we could enter that way without being immediately caught.

Sneaking in through the back door on the opposite side was a much better idea. Luckily for us, when I tried the handle, it wasn't locked.

Even from the outside, the gymnasium looked too real to be a replica. If Grayfia turned around later and told me that this had been the real Kuou Academy all along, I would completely believe her.

Koneko and I entered from the back, behind the stage. The curtains were drawn, so we had a full view of the inside of the hall.

I scanned the area from one corner. That's when Koneko murmured, "…Enemies. Nearby."

—!

But before I had time to register my own surprise, a voice echoed through the hall. "We know you're there, servants of Gremory! We've been waiting for you to show your faces."

It was a woman's voice—one of Riser's servants! They must have been waiting for us!

In that case, there was no point in hiding any longer.

Koneko and I stepped out onto the stage. In the middle of the hall stood four demon women.

There was the older woman wearing a Chinese dress, the pair of twins, and the petite girl who'd beaten me up last time. I had really been hoping I wouldn't bump into her again so soon.

If I remembered correctly, the one in the Chinese dress was a Rook. The twins were Pawns, as was the petite girl. I knew this only because we'd taken a look at a photograph of all of Riser's Familia members before the match.

Three Pawns and a Rook... Given that Koneko and I amounted to only one Rook and one Pawn respectively, we were at a clear numerical disadvantage.

Still, an encounter here was unavoidable if we were to carry out our plan.

"Boosted Gear, stand by!"

"Boost!"

Wasting no time, I began doubling my power. *I can do this!* I told myself.

"...Issei, you take the Pawns. I'll handle the Rook."

"Right!"

Koneko and I both faced our respective opponents. The woman in the Chinese dress adopted a martial-arts pose, and the petite girl brandished her staff. The twins readied a pair of handheld chain saws, and with beaming grins—

Hold on, chain saws?!

Vroooooooooom! The mechanical weapons let out terrifying sounds.

What?! Are they serious?! Surely, something like that is too dangerous to bring to a fight, right?!

"Dismemberment time!" they sang in gleeful unison.

Saying something like that so cheerfully should've been illegal! I didn't want to be cut into pieces. Letting them reach me was out of the question.

Crash! Bang!

A short distance away, Koneko and the woman in the Chinese dress had already begun exchanging blows.

They threw punch after punch at each other, and the fight quickly became a martial-arts contest. They were both Rooks, so each one of those hits must have carried tremendous force. I had assumed that Koneko, with her small frame, would have the advantage when it came to movement, but her opponent was no slouch, either, lightly launching into one attack after another.

Whoosh!

The petite Pawn girl swung her staff around dramatically. Her name was Milla, if I was remembering correctly.

Bitter memories flashed through the back of my mind. I had acted all confident and self-assured and had been soundly defeated without even having delivered a single blow... Things were going to go differently this time!

"Cut! Cut! Cut! Cut! Cut!"

The twins were coming right at me, dragging their chain saws along the floor!

Vroooooooooom! A chain saw roared in my ear as it passed by. *Argh! Too close!* They almost cut my head clean off!

I sent one of the twins flying with a shoulder tackle and put some space between myself and the other one. A simple move like that was unlikely to cause my Boosted Gear to reset, but if I got carried away and did something flashy, I risked losing all my increased power.

Swoosh!

Something came flying toward me from behind.

"Uh-oh!"

I managed to dodge that, too, though only by a hairbreadth. Milla's club passed right by my flank!

Yes, I dodged it!

I was moving faster than even I had expected! Whether it was the result of my training or something brought on by Rias lifting the seal earlier, I couldn't say for certain.

Either way, this was my chance! I was going to show everyone what I could do!

Unfortunately, at that moment of overconfidence, the edge of a chain saw grazed my cheek! It hurt, but more than that, it sent blood flying. My uniform had been torn as well. That was a close one.

"Boost!"

It was time for my second power-up! Clearly, my opponents weren't willing to wait as I charged up. They moved in to attack again, but...

"Ha!" I turned my body sideways to dodge the attack coming from up above, leaped back to dodge the next vertical attack, and then ducked down! I caught the final strike from Milla's staff head-on by crossing my arms!

All right! How's that for a perfect defense?!

"Argh, stop moving!"

"Why can't we hit him?!"

The chain saw–wielding twins stamped their feet in frustration.

"...We can't break his guard," Milla said. She certainly didn't seem pleased to find that her attacks were now ineffective.

Too bad for you, I thought. I'd really given training my best effort. Facing the prez and the others would've been impossible if I got my ass kicked all over again!

"Boost!"

This was it! My third power-up! I was ready!

"Let's go, Sacred Gear!"

"Explosion!"

Now that I had reached this stage, I was ready to fight for real. My whole body was overflowing with energy. I couldn't afford to waste even a single moment of my temporary power-up!

"I'll deal with you two first!" With surprising speed, I bolted toward the twins. This might sound a little conceited coming from me, but it was a damn impressive sprint.

My enhanced movements left my enemy Pawns little time to react. Realizing her predicament, the first of the twins swung her chain saw wildly, but my fist was faster!

Bang!

I sent the first of that chain saw–wielding pair flying.

"How dare you hit my sister!"

The other twin pointed her chain saw in my direction, but I twisted my body backward and struck her with a powerful backhand blow. She fell to the floor with a *thud*.

"Argh!"

The staff-wielding girl lunged toward me with her weapon. It was the same sort of attack she'd used to one-shot me in our last encounter, but I wasn't about to let that happen again!

I spun around to dodge her thrust. As I did so, an opening revealed itself as Milla followed through, her attack striking only the empty air. This was my chance!

"Take that!" I cried.

Crack!

I struck out with the side of my hand, cleaving right through Milla's staff. My hand throbbed with pain. Evidently, that thing had been a lot stronger than it looked.

Before she had a chance to respond, I threw my now-disarmed opponent to the ground.

"Gyah!" The girl let out a loud scream as she rolled across the ground.

"Ngh!" The strained cry through gritted teeth belonged to the woman in the Chinese dress. I glanced around, only to find her lying on the floor and holding herself up with her hands. Meanwhile, Koneko towered above the other Rook, still maintaining her fighting stance.

Whoa. It was obvious, even from a cursory glance, that Koneko was the stronger fighter.

"Riser will be mad if we lose to a guy like this!" spat one of the chain-saw twins, having climbed back to her feet.

"We'll cut you to pieces!" the other twin declared as she restarted her chain saw.

Heh-heh… Get as worked up as you want, but the preparations for my victory are already complete. It was time for my ultimate technique.

"Have a taste of my new special move! Dress Break!"

Snap!

With a snap of my fingers, the chain saw–wielding twins and the girl with the staff each had her clothes get blown away.

Yep, even their underwear was sent flying! Their pale, curvaceous bodies stood bare before me. All three of them were a little under-developed, but it was still a feast for the eyes.

Snort!

Blood started gushing down my nose as I broke into a huge grin.

"E-eeeeeeeek!"

The girls' screams echoed throughout the gymnasium. All three of them crouched low to the ground, trying to hide their private parts.

"Aha! How do you like my ultimate technique, Dress Break?! All I had to do was keep imagining your clothes being torn right off and dedicate my demonic abilities to stripping you naked!"

Yep, I had just poured all my powers into this ultimate move. I didn't have much in the way of demonic power to begin with, so even though I spent nearly every waking moment thinking about lewd stuff like this, the technique still took everything I had.

There was no arguing with the results, though. It was a marvel to behold!

Look upon my Works, ye Mighty, and despair!

This was why I'd spent all that time peeling vegetables and fruit using nothing more than my demonic powers. I'd peel them until I thought my mind was starting to slip.

For the technique to work, I first needed to come into physical contact with my target. At that moment, I then had to pour my demonic powers into them. The end result spoke for itself.

"You're the worst! The enemy of all women!"

"You're an animal! A lecherous fiend!"

The chain saw–wielding twins launched indignant insults at me. I gladly accepted their words, though.

"…I misjudged you." Koneko's cold murmur, however, stabbed at my heart.

At that moment, a voice sounded from the transceiver in my ear. *"Issei, Koneko. Can you hear me?"*

It was the prez. It looked like Koneko was listening in, too.

"Yep! We're both fine! We're just about ready!" I replied.

"Very good. Akeno has finished her preparations. You know what to do!"

It was time! Koneko and I glanced at each other, exchanging brief nods.

Paying no heed to our opponents crouching down on the floor, the two of us sped toward the entrance.

"Cowards!" Riser's servants called out behind us. "This is an important strategic position!"

They weren't wrong. The gymnasium connected the new school building to the old one. Had this been a real game of chess, it would've been the center of the board. That made controlling it absolutely vital. That's precisely why we had gathered the four of them in there! That had been our plan all along! Koneko and I had basically been decoys!

Just as the two of us exited the building…

Flash!

There was a blinding burst of light.

Boooooooooom!

A huge pillar of lightning crashed down into the center of the gymnasium with a deafening roar.

By the time things settled down, the building had been reduced to rubble.

"Take that," came Akeno's voice.

Above us, Akeno was floating in the air, her black wings spread, staring down at the destruction with a look of pure gratification. Her right hand was held up high above her, and sparks of electricity were dancing around it.

"Three of Lord Riser's Pawns and one of his Rooks have been retired." Grayfia's voice echoed across the battlefield.

Hold on—that one strike knocked out all four of our opponents just now?! Seriously?!

That's when I recalled something Kiba had mentioned to me a while ago: "There are some who call Akeno the Vestal of Thunder. Since the president isn't old enough yet to have played in any official Rating Games, Akeno isn't exactly famous, but she *is* well-known among a certain group of enthusiasts."

The Vestal of Thunder... Talk about terrifying. If she had hit me with that attack, I definitely would've croaked on the spot.

I made a mental note to never cross her.

"We did it, Koneko!" I tried to pat her on the shoulder, but she shrank back.

"...Don't touch me...," she hissed, glaring daggers.

A disappointing reaction, though I had to admit it was an understandable one. Anyone would've been wary after seeing my ultimate technique.

"Ha-ha, don't worry. I won't use that move against my allies," I reassured her.

"...It's still disgusting."

It looked like she well and truly hated me now...

"Everyone, can you hear me? Akeno just delivered a flashy finishing

move. You've all successfully pulled off the first stage of our strategy."
Rias's voice came through the transceiver. She sounded pleased.

This had all been part of her overall plan.

Destroying the gymnasium had been an important first step, so long as we could ensnare several members of Riser's Familia in it.

Koneko and I had entered from the back entrance, but that had actually been a ruse. We'd known that Riser's side would be monitoring the building and that as soon as we got inside, they would attack. All we had to do was keep them occupied for a short while and then make our escape. As soon as we were out of range, Akeno had demolished the whole building from the sky.

We had been the bait to lure our opponents into our trap. Having accomplished that, we fell back and left the rest to Akeno.

Rias's strategy had gone exactly as planned. We had abandoned a strategically valuable location and used it as part of our attack. The trick had allowed us to remove three Pawns and one Rook, all without losing a single member of our own team. What could've been better than that?

"Now that she's used it once, Akeno's lightning attack will take time to charge before it can be used again. We can't rely on her for a rapid-fire assault. Moreover, the other side still outnumbers us. I will depart once she is ready to use it again. Until that time, I'll leave the rest to you. Move on to the next phase!" Rias instructed.

"Right!" I replied.

With the prez and Asia moving out, the next order of business for Koneko and me was to join up with Kiba and engage the enemy on the athletic track!

Just as we were about to head over, however...

Booooom!

There was an ear-rending sound like that of an explosion, and at its source—

"...K-Koneko!"

The petite girl was lying sprawled on the ground, and smoke was rising up from her body. I hurried to her side and took the girl in my arms.

Her uniform was in tatters, as if she'd been caught in an explosion. Several pieces of her outfit had completely disappeared. Something about that noise reminded me of—

"Take *that*," a mysterious voice mocked.

Up in the sky floated a figure, wings spread wide. She was clad in some kind of mage's outfit, and her face was hidden behind a hood. It was clearly one of Riser's servants, and she'd just taken out Koneko!

Hold on. Isn't that Riser's Queen?! We'd just run into that bastard's strongest piece!

"Fu-fu-fu. The best moment to move in on your prey is when they lower their guard after a minor victory. Sacrificing a few of our many members is perfectly acceptable if it means capturing some of yours in return. You are simply too few. Just this one loss will leave you incapacitated, no? Even if you manage to rout us, you can't hope to defeat Master Riser. You were better off quitting before you began." The woman let out a mirth-filled laugh.

"...Issei... Akeno...," Koneko murmured weakly, her voice about to give out. "...I'm sorry... I wish I could have been more useful..."

"Th-there's no need to apologize. You did everything you were supposed to. Just hold on! Once Asia gets here, she'll have you up and—"

Before I could finish, a bright light suddenly enveloped Koneko's body. She turned transparent for a moment before completely disappearing.

...

"*Lady Rias Gremory's Rook has been retired,*" sounded Grayfia's impassive voice.

Before the match, Rias had explained that if any of us sustained enough damage that we were no longer able to fight, we would automatically be retired from the match. When that happened, we would be transported to a place where we could receive medical attention.

That was why it wasn't a huge problem if anyone got too beaten up. No one actually died in Rating Games. Those four members of Riser's Familia who Akeno had defeated a moment ago had no doubt been transported to the same place as Koneko.

I knew that. I understood that. It was all a kind of mock battle, but even so, it was just a little too much... When Koneko vanished from my arms, I could still feel the phantom of her weight.

Damn it! My whole body began trembling with rage.

"Get down here! I'll crush you!" I called out in provocation at Riser's Queen, completely throwing the next stage of our plan to the wind.

Even I knew it was an ill-advised course of action, but I didn't care. I couldn't forgive her. Koneko was in tears the moment she disappeared, tears of anguish and regret! She should've still been able to fight!

Damn it! If I'd seen Riser's Queen coming even a moment earlier, I might have been able to save her! But I just had to let the success of the first phase of our plan go to my head!

"Fu-fu-fu. You're a bold little Pawn, aren't you, boy? Shall I destroy you like I did that other girl just now?" The mage turned her arm toward me. She was going to attack again!

"Oh dear. I'm your opponent here, Miss Yubelluna, Queen of Riser Phenex. Or should I call you the Bomb Queen?" Akeno asked as she placed herself between us, as if to shield me.

"I don't like that name, Vestal of Thunder. It leaves a bad taste in my mouth. I've been looking forward to fighting you."

"Issei, go and find Yuuto. I'll take care of things here."

"B-but—!" I began to protest, but for the first time that I could remember, Akeno's expression as she stared back at me turned stern. My heart skipped a beat. I could feel the icy sting of her glare.

"Issei, you have your own role to play. Now, go. This is my job."

She was right, of course. I would just get in her way. I had to see to the tasks that only I could perform. There was little else to do but grit my teeth in frustration.

At this, Akeno returned to her usual peaceful smile. "Don't worry. I'll avenge Koneko. I'll pour my soul into destroying this Queen!"

—!

A golden aura wrapped itself around Akeno's body. It was her demonic power. One look at Akeno in that moment was all it took to know how powerful she was. Rias's Queen was the strongest of all the members of her Familia, after all.

"Akeno! I'll leave this to you!" I called out and took off to find Kiba at the athletic track.

A moment later, a tremendous blast of thunder ripped through the air behind me.

The battle had moved into its middle phase.

Life.5
The Acclaimed Battle Continues!

I hurried toward the athletic track to join up with Kiba.

"Three of Lord Riser Phenex's Pawns have been retired."

Another announcement! It sounded like someone defeated three more members of his Familia!

The question was, who? I was still on the move, Akeno was engaged with Riser's Queen, and the prez and Asia should have been en route to their next target. It could have only been Kiba!

If Riser had lost seven pieces, then he had another nine left, including himself. We had lost Koneko, which left us with five. We were still at a disadvantage!

Out of nowhere, someone grabbed my arm. *An enemy?!* I thought. I was a long way off from the athletic track. I braced myself for the worst, only to find that it was Kiba. He was wearing his usual disarming smile.

"Huh? Oh, it's you," I said.

"Yep."

It looked like he'd been keeping an eye on events at the athletic track from a safe distance, behind the storage building at the edge of the grounds.

"Sorry, Kiba. Koneko…"

"I know. I heard the announcement. It's a shame. I can never really tell what she's thinking, but she was putting her all into this match. She went over and beyond when we set our traps in the forest."

"…We'll win this."

"Of course we will, Issei."

We bumped our fists together. Kiba might have been an accursed pretty boy during regular school life, but here on the battlefield, he was the best of allies.

We were the two male members of the Occult Research Club. If we failed to prove our worth here, there was no way we would be able to show our faces to the girls!

"Was it you who took down three of their Pawns?" I asked.

Kiba nodded. "Yeah. The clubhouses next to the athletic grounds are a strategic area. It was only natural that our enemies would want to occupy them. All I did was lure out the Pawns who they had on lookout and round them up. Their boss kept her cool and didn't respond, though. I guess she used the Pawns to evaluate how I would attack. It looks like Riser Phenex doesn't mind sacrificing his pieces so long as it gives him an advantage. But he can only take that approach thanks to the size of his Familia and his own immortality, of course." The corners of Kiba's mouth rose up in a faint grin, but his eyes remained serious. "He's deployed a Knight, a Rook, and a Bishop out there. Three pieces in total."

"…That leaves us badly outnumbered…," I muttered.

"Well, it just goes to show how much they don't want us taking it. Now that we've destroyed the gymnasium, this is the logical place to gather our forces."

Kiba had a point. The gymnasium and the athletic grounds were the two main routes between the old and the new school buildings. With one of those avenues already eliminated, the only place that needed guarding against was this one.

It was a natural move to concentrate one's forces there. Although it was true that our attack on the gymnasium had forced their Queen to the front line.

By the look of things, our battle at the athletic grounds was shaking up to be way more intense than the one at the gymnasium. I was kind of scared!

"Are you feeling nervous?" Kiba asked with a smile.

I felt my cheeks flushing. "O-of course I am! I barely have any combat experience, and I've been thrown into the deep end! Compared to everything you've been through, I'm a small fry!"

I did have the Boosted Gear, and that counted for something, but it didn't exactly mean much with me as its user. It really was a useless treasure.

Even if it was, I'd already made up my mind to fight for Rias. I had to do *something* for her.

No matter how weak I was on the field, I wasn't going to let anyone take me down without a fight. If I was going to be defeated, I wanted to at least take as many of them as I could with me. That oath had been etched into my heart.

"Look here," Kiba said, showing me his hands.

—! They were shaking.

"You said I have a lot of combat experience, Issei. That may be true, but this is still my first time in a Rating Game—a genuine battle between two teams of demons. While this may be a unique situation, we're still fighting for real. We're going to have to do this again countless times down the line, but this is our first game. We can't afford to give our opponents even a single opening. As the president's Familia, we have to do everything we can, because this is a pivotal moment for us all, something that will stick with us into the future. It's a joyous thing, but it's also terrifying. I certainly won't forget how badly my hands are trembling. This nervousness and tension will become a source of nourishment, and I'll use it to better myself. We both have to grow stronger, Issei."

Kiba... It sounded like he had been thinking long and hard about all this... He really was dedicated when it came to combat.

"In that case, let's show the girls what this pairing is capable of!" I declared.

"Ha-ha! Does that make me the *top*, then?"

"I'm the top, you idiot! No, wait, I mean—! Argh, damn you, pretty boy!"

He'd managed to get me completely pulled into this rhythm! Ugh, what was I doing?!

At that moment, a loud, inspired voice rang out: "I am Karlamine, Knight to Master Riser! I tire of us trying to probe each other's tactics! Knight of Rias Gremory, what do you say we settle this sword-to-sword?"

A woman clad in a full suit of armor strode gallantly out onto the baseball pitch.

What boldness! She would've had no excuse if someone picked her off from behind!

"Heh," Kiba chuckled. "Now that she's given her name, on my honor as a swordsman, I'll have to reveal myself," he murmured before striding out of the shadows of the storage building.

He was heading straight for the baseball pitch.

"That idiot," I muttered in complaint, though I trailed along after him nonetheless.

He is pretty cool, though, I thought as I watched him from behind.

"I am Yuuto Kiba, Knight to Rias Gremory."

"And I'm Issei Hyoudou, her Pawn!"

The two of us gave our names to the enemy Knight named Karlamine.

The female Knight flashed us a joyous smile. "I'm glad to see that Rias Gremory's Familia boasts at least two honorable warriors. Although I do question your sanity, coming out to face me directly."

Hey, come on, now. Is she calling us crazy?

"But I do adore fools like you two. Shall we begin?" With that, Karlamine drew her sword from her scabbard.

Kiba readied his blade, too. "A duel between two Knights—I've been looking forward to this. It's been a while since I had a proper bout," he responded defiantly.

Judging by that grin of his, he wasn't lying!

"Well said, Knight of Rias Gremory!" Karlamine leaped into action, her attack flying toward Kiba as if she was launching into a dance.

Clash!

Sparks flew wildly as their blades made contact! Perhaps because they were both Knights, their movements were unbelievably fast.

The fight had only just started, but their swords moved swifter than my eyes could perceive! Kiba and Karlamine both kept appearing and disappearing in different spots across the field.

What am I supposed to do exactly? It would've been tactless of me to try to help Kiba. He was in the middle of a one-on-one duel, after all.

Hmm, maybe I should try to encourage him? I wondered.

"You look bored."

"—!"

I spun around, only to find a woman approaching who had half her face hidden behind a mask. As I recalled, she was a Rook. The very next instant, another figure appeared.

"Good grief, I can't stand people like that. All they ever think about is swords, swords, swords. And did you see that face Karlamine pulled when we sacrificed the Pawns? You would think she doesn't approve of Lord Riser's strategy. And now she's gone and found a cute little boy who shares her fetish for swinging a sword around."

This new beauty, openly voicing her complaints, was wearing a dress like that of a European princess. Her hair was bound up on both sides of her head in intricate braids. She really did give off a regal sort of presence.

Apparently, we'd been surrounded by the lookouts who Riser had dispatched to the athletic grounds.

The Bishop was staring at me with half-lidded eyes.

Wh-what is it? I thought.

"Hmm. So you're the Pawn Lady Rias Gremory keeps fawning over? She has a strange sense of taste, that one."

How dare she speak so rudely about the prez! Ugh! She may have had a pretty face, but she had a poison tongue!

I leaped to a safe distance and readied myself against these two opponents.

"Boosted Gear, stand by!"

"Boost!"

I started powering up my Sacred Gear. I had no choice but to leave the Knight to Kiba and take on these two myself!

The princess-like Bishop, however, let out an exasperated sigh. "I won't fight you. Isabella, why don't you take him?"

The masked woman, Isabella, nodded. Her companion withdrew to the sidelines.

What's with this? Her Highness doesn't feel like fighting?!

"That was always our plan. Why don't we pass the time together?"

"Ah, sure. That's fine and all, but what about that Bishop?" I asked.

I could hardly believe she wasn't in the mood to fight. Wasn't this an important game for her side? I had no idea what to do, faced with an opponent who had practically abandoned the match.

The masked woman placed a hand on her forehead, her expression troubled. "Ah, don't worry about her. She's *unique*. For the most part, she'll just be watching."

"Wh-what's that supposed to mean?!" I blurted out.

Spectating shouldn't have been an option! Did this Rating Game not matter to them?

"She's— Well, that's Ravel Phenex, Master Riser's younger sister. She only joined Master Riser's Familia because of a special circumstance, but she's still his blood sister."

...Huh? That beauty right there is Riser's sister? That bird bastard's? Huh? Huuuuuuuuuuuh?!

She waved to me from a good distance away, as if amused by my sudden realization.

It didn't feel real. Not only had Riser let his younger sister join his Familia, but he let her fight in his battles?!

"Master Riser has a certain take on it. *'There's a social meaning to having your sister in your harem. I mean, it's incestuous, right? There are a lot of people out there who dig that kind of thing. I'm not into sisters, though, so it's more for show than anything else.'* That's how he put it, if I'm not mistaken."

That jackass really was a total pervert! Still, I could understand why he might've wanted to have his sister in his harem. I definitely wished I had a younger sister.

No, stop it! I shook my head. *She's his sister, and that's why she isn't going to fight. Fine by me!*

"Let's do this, Pawn of Rias Gremory!" Isabella called out.

Whoosh!

The masked woman lunged forward, her fist brushing past my cheek as she threw a punch.

Wha—?! Luckily, I shifted to the side by pure reflex!

"Hmm. So you can dodge moves like that. My apologies. I should have given you more credit. Let's step this up a notch or two!"

Her body swayed strangely from left to right for a second, and then…

Whoosh! Slam!

Isabella launched into a flurry of unbelievable attacks from all sorts of impossible angles! *Whoa!* No sooner had I dodged an elbow strike than Isabella's hand lashed out toward me like a whip!

Is this one of those flicker jabs used in boxing?! Something like that was sure to hurt if it connected.

I couldn't launch into a counterattack of my own until the Boosted Gear was sufficiently powered up! It was all I could do to stay on the defensive. I desperately fought to avoid her attacks.

Thud!

"…Gah!"

An intense pain tore through my abdomen. That Isabella had kicked me! I'd been so preoccupied with her punches that I hadn't been paying attention to what she was doing with her legs! The strike threw me off balance, and her next move was coming straight for my face!

A combination move of those flicker jabs pounded my head. Believe me when I say it really hurt!

"Boost!"

That was my fifth boost. Five increases probably would've been enough if I'd been facing another Pawn, but they still weren't enough to take on a Rook. Rooks were second only to Queens in value, after all. I couldn't afford to risk any attack that wasn't going to be enough!

Despite crossing my arms to guard against the flurry of blows, each strike still carried an immense force behind it. If this kept up, I was going to be retired in no time!

Seizing on a break in her flicker jabs, I threw myself backward.

Isabella's attacks finally came to a stop, but still she was maintaining a light footing. There was no telling when she might launch into another barrage.

Thank goodness for all those sparring sessions with Kiba and Koneko! They'd really proven their worth. Now I knew how to discern when my opponent was about to cease their attacks. What's more, Rias had taught me how to escape, which had enabled me to safely get some distance.

The Rook broke into a grin. "I underestimated you. To tell you the truth, I expected that kick to be the end… Rias Gremory has trained you well. Your physical endurance is impressive."

My "physical endurance"? *Is it really that good?*

"In a serious battle, the most important thing of all is your stamina. Any idiot can fight, but it takes considerable fortitude to keep going beyond a couple of minutes. Combat requires physical strength and mental fortitude. Just avoiding your opponent's attacks takes significant effort. The fact that you can do so speaks to long hours of physical training."

—! My chest tightened.

All that arduous training and Rias's many cruel demands. Suffering through those early-morning marathons and carrying boulders up the mountain had made me feel like I was going to die. Admittedly, I'd had doubts about whether it was really doing any good, but Rias never gave up and stayed by my side through it all.

My eyes grew moist. Before I knew it, I was shedding tears in front of my opponent.

Prez! I can fight on my own now! All your efforts have paid off!

Losing couldn't have been further from my mind at that point. I was going to win this whole thing for Rias! Some Rook in my way wasn't going to stop me!

"...Perhaps I said too much. You seem emboldened," Isabella remarked.

"Rook Isabella. I'm the weakest member of Rias Gremory's Familia, and I don't have much combat experience... But I'm still going to defeat you!" I declared with confidence.

Whoosh!

A sword cut through the air. It was the sound of Kiba's weapon, the Holy Eraser. His Sacred Gear took the form of a sword wrapped in darkness, and it consumed light. Despite being up against such a strong weapon, the other Knight seemed to have managed to deflect it and send the blade flying from its hilt.

"I'm afraid your Sacred Gear will not work against me," Karlamine quipped.

I couldn't tell if her sword was wreathed in flame or was made of fire itself, I wasn't sure. Whatever the case, it looked to have beaten Kiba's.

However, Kiba, far from shrinking back, flashed her a dauntless grin. "Then I have something to tell you, too. Unfortunately, that isn't all my Sacred Gear is capable of."

"What? Nonsense. Knight of the House of Gremory, it is beneath the dignity of a swordsman to—"

"Freeze," Kiba said with a low growl. At that moment, something began to gather around his now-bladeless sword.

Huh? I felt a sudden chill… A wave of frigid air began to blow.

At that moment, Kiba's sword started to freeze. Ice gathered at its hilt, expanding outward into the shape of a blade.

Crack!

With a shattering sound, Kiba's sword changed into a weapon of crystalline ice.

"Any manner of flame will perish in the face of my sword—Flame Deleter!" Kiba declared.

A-a frozen sword?! So Kiba's Sacred Gear isn't just a blade of darkness?!

Everyone except Kiba looked utterly amazed, though that was to be expected. To me it seemed like that pretty boy had just done the impossible!

"A-absurd! Are you telling me you have *two* Sacred Gears?!" Karlamine loosed a horizonal slash with her burning weapon, her face filled with frustration and bewilderment.

C-c-crack…

The moment her flame sword met Kiba's frigid one, it was engulfed in ice. With an echoing sound, the enemy Knight's weapon shattered.

Despite such a loss, Karlamine didn't let off her attacks. She cast her broken weapon aside, unsheathing a fresh short sword from her hip. Raising it to the sky, she declared, "We, the proud servants of the House of Phenex, reign supreme over the elements of wind, flame, and life itself! Let's see how you endure this blazing vortex!"

Roooooaaaaar!

A roiling whirlwind of red-hot flames began to swirl in the middle of the baseball pitch, centered around Karlamine. The blistering air was already searing my skin.

"That lunatic! Has she forgotten that her own allies are still here, too?!" Isabella spat as she raised her arms to shield her face.

The hot blast of air began to melt Kiba's ice sword, yet Kiba himself remained unfazed.

"I see. So you're trying to smother us with heat… But I'm afraid you're going to have to..." He paused there, holding his once again bladeless sword in front of him, then declared in a powerful tone, "... Stop."

Whoosh!

With a thundering sound, the torrent of flame was sucked right into the hilt of Kiba's sword. After a few seconds, the wind ceased, and the baseball pitch was silent again.

"Repression Calm. It's been a while since I've had to use more than two swords in one battle."

In his hand, Kiba gripped a unique, circular sort of edged weapon. A strange, seemingly impossible cyclone was rotating in the center of it. I had to wonder if he'd just somehow captured Karlamine's fire-vortex attack?

Since when does he have a sword like that?!

"...Multiple Sacred Gears? Don't tell me you steal the Sacred Gears of others and make them your own?" Karlamine asked, incredulous.

Kiba, however, shook his head. "I don't have multiple Sacred Gears, nor have I acquired any extra ones. I forge them myself."

"You...forge them?"

"Indeed. Sword Birth—the ability to forge all manner of demonic blades. That is the true name of my Sacred Gear. This is what it's capable of."

As Kiba turned his palm to the ground, multiple swords stabbed into the earth, each a different size and shape. If what he had just said was true, they were all distinct demonic swords!

"Boost!"

This was it, 150 seconds exactly! I was ready!

I gathered a mass of power in my hand, shaped it into the first image that came to mind, and unleashed!

Rias's advice sounded in the back of my mind. The easiest way for me to use my power was to focus on the most destructive thing imaginable. In my case, that was Satoru Soramago's Dragon Wave attack from the series *Dragon Orb!*

"Boosted Gear! Now!"

"Explosion!"

A massive ball of energy accumulated in my palms. I extended both hands outward, the one on top of the other, and imagined myself unleashing a blast of raw energy as the power flowed through me.

Even when using this attack, I had to play it carefully. It wouldn't do if I unleashed the same level of power that had destroyed that mountain back during our training camp. If I destroyed the new school building, the prez's plan would be thrown into disarray. I had to restrain myself as much as possible…

Ultimate move! Dragon Shot! I screamed in my mind.

Boom!

A torrent of demonic power burst forth from my outstretched hands.

"Gah!"

The force of the blast threw me backward. The blinding light that erupted out of my palms flooded my eyes.

It was huge!

That mass of power had to have been at least five times the size of my own body. It coursed toward Riser's Rook at a tremendous speed.

Rias had said that the most troubling piece in a Rating Game was always the Rook. That was because they possessed such high levels of both offensive and defensive potential. While that might've made the piece sound kind of plain, such abilities were still pretty terrifying. It was most common for a demon to assign the role of Rook to someone who already possessed considerable skills in those areas; however, there were those who adopted other strategies, too.

For instance, there were those demons who gave their Rook pieces to individuals with high levels of demonic power or incredible speed.

Those who specialized in demonic magic tended to have weak physical constitutions. Being assigned the attributes of a Rook could compensate for that weakness. Similarly, granting the role to someone who was already swift on their feet resulted in a high-level jack-of-all-trades.

Above all, Rooks possessed a special technique similar to a Pawn's Promotion move: Castling.

They could switch positions with their King at any instant. According to Rias, this was their most troubling ability. It couldn't be used if the King was currently in check, but it was still a formidable skill to have. Whether to increase their latent abilities or to compensate for their weaknesses was up to the leader of the Familia, but there were countless ways of making use of a Rook.

That was why I had to take down the one in front of me with a single shot!

"Isabella! Don't try to counter it! Run!" Riser's Knight Karlamine screamed.

Isabella, who it seemed had been about to try to meet the attack, instead leaped to safety.

Whoosh!

She managed to avoid the blast just in time. My Dragon Shot, having missed its target, flew off into the distance. It was barreling straight for a replica of the school's tennis courts.

Booooooooooom!

A deafening sound shook the earth! There was a brilliant red flash, followed by a buffeting blast of wind!

When the dust settled, I turned back to the tennis courts, my eyes opening wide in surprise. They were gone! The tennis courts, along with the surrounding parts of the athletic track, had been completely obliterated!

Did I do that with just one blow?! Even if it was a replica, that single attack had completely destroyed a portion of the school grounds. Nothing remained of the tennis courts but a huge crater! Even though I'd tried to restrain the power of my attack, it had still been extremely devastating!

Yet again, I was forced to acknowledge just how insane my Sacred Gear was.

"Isabella! Take down that Pawn! His Sacred Gear has the power to turn the tide of the match!" Karlamine cried out from across the battlefield.

At that instruction, Riser's Rook set her sights on me. "Understood! We can't afford to let you get a Promotion with that Boosted Gear of yours! I'll take you down first!"

Sorry to say, but I'm not the same fighter I was a moment ago, Isabella! At this level, I'm as strong as a high-class demon!

She came flying toward me, launching into a punch and a flurry of kicks. Even in the face of such a barrage, I held firm against each blow, concentrating my energy into my left arm all the while.

"Tch!"

I countered, hurling my fist toward Isabella. She crossed her arms, hoping to shield herself, and yet—

Wham!

The weight of my swing broke through her guard, sending the masked Rook flying!

All right! I thought. *I made physical contact!* That meant I could use one of my other skills.

"Burst! Dress Break!"

Fwoosh!

At that moment, Isabella's clothes blew clean off, revealing her dewy, naked body. Her breasts were *huge!* Her well-toned body was so fit and tight! I made sure to burn the image into my memory!

"Wha—?! What have you done?!" She reflexively covered herself with her hands as best she could.

That was exactly the sort of reaction I'd been expecting.

This was it! Without a moment's delay, I gathered a small mass of demonic power in my right hand and imagined myself hurling it toward her!

"Go!"

Whoom!

That wave of energy built up tremendous force as it sped toward its mark!

"Ugh! How can you—?!"

The burst of energy enveloped Isabella before she had a chance to answer.

Booooom!

A huge shock wave rippled outward. By the time the vibrations subsided, Isabella was lying flat on the ground, her body encased in a glowing aura. Slowly, she turned transparent before disappearing altogether.

"Reset."

My Boosted Gear had reached its limit.

"One of Lord Riser Phenex's Rooks has been retired," echoed Grayfia's voice.

"All right!" I cried with joy at having defeated such a powerful opponent.

I'd really proven myself a capable fighter, and I had those long hours training with the prez to thank for it!

Having settled my fight with Isabella, I paused to catch my breath.

I had used up a lot of both physical stamina and demonic power. Attacks like my Dragon Shot were really possible only by drawing out the latent energy within me. So the stronger my attack was, the more exhausted I became.

I was content being at a level of using that move two more times, but I had the feeling that a third use of it was bound to leave me so weak that I'd likely faint on the spot. I didn't trust myself to get off more than one more shot. I was going to have to be careful going forward.

With Isabella defeated, Karlamine snickered at me. "It looks like both Isabella and I underestimated that Pawn and his Boosted Gear. It was unwise to think of him as an ordinary foot soldier."

Is she praising me? If so, I had no complaint. Her words filled me with a touch of pride, actually.

"But that is a cruel technique—stripping away a woman's clothes…"

"It *is* rather undignified… Our Issei is a bit of a pervert. Allow me to apologize on his behalf," Kiba said.

Hearing him apologize was a little surprising. I didn't quite know how to respond to that.

"But a wielder of Demon Swords… What good fortune," Karlamine said, holding her short sword with a backhand grip. "It seems I'm fated to do battle with swordsmen armed with unique weapons."

"Oh? You've fought against other Demon Swords?" Kiba asked with clear curiosity.

"Not a Demon Sword. A Holy Sword."

"—!" At this, Kiba's expression changed to one of unbelievable bloodlust. Seriously, he looked like some kind of murderer! A horrible, chilling aura filled the air. My whole body was shivering.

There was a frigid glint to Kiba's eyes. "Tell me about the wielder of this Holy Sword," he said, his voice almost imperceptibly low.

What terrifying hostility. He was just as petrifying as the prez when she got angry.

A Holy Sword? I thought. *What does that have to do with anything?*

"Oh, do you know him? But I'm afraid we're both swordsmen, you and I. Words are not enough. My blade will be the one to answer your question!"

"…I see… In that case, so long as you can still talk, it doesn't matter if I send you to the brink of death."

Wha—?!

A savage animosity emanated from the two fighters that was so powerful, it made the earth shake and my skin crawl.

Kiba! What's come over you? What happened to that refreshing smile of yours?!

Overwhelmed by his change in personality, I almost didn't notice the several newcomers approaching.

"Here they are."

"Huh? What happened to Isabella?"

"Don't tell me she lost?"

Other members of Riser's Familia had begun to show up. I remembered their faces. There were two Pawns, one Bishop, one Knight... Hold on, was that all of them?

Uh-oh. Did they want to stage a massive battle here or something? It was just Kiba and me!

Akeno was probably still busy dealing with the Queen. Every now and then, I could catch the sound of powerful thunderclaps echoing through the sky.

As for the prez and Asia... Well, I had no idea where they were. Had they still been following the plan, they should've left the headquarters.

"Hey, you there, Pawn!" one of Riser's servants called out.

What now? I grimaced.

"Master Riser said he's going to fight your dear princess one-on-one. See?" The girl pointed to a place high above.

Turning in that direction, I spotted a figure with raging wings of flame and another with a pitch-black pair on the roof of the new school building.

The figure with the black wings had crimson hair! It was Rias!

"Issei! Can you hear me, Issei?!" came Asia's voice through my earpiece.

"Asia?! What happened? What's the prez doing?"

"We're both on top of the school building. Riser challenged her to a duel, and she accepted! That's how we managed to reach here without any trouble, but now..."

What's her goal here? I had no idea what I was supposed to do.

Seeing my consternation, Riser's sister called out to me, her lips curling in a cutting grin. "My brother must be in a good mood, seeing as how well we're doing. He's probably taking pity on Lady Rias. After all, we would've obviously won if the game had continued like normal. At this rate, you'd have all been defeated before he ever got a turn himself!"

Riser's sister—Ravel—covered her mouth with her hand as she let out a shrill guffaw.

Ugh, she was starting to get on my nerves!

"The prez is strong! And Akeno will go help her as soon as she takes down your Queen! Not only that, but Kiba will take you all down with his Demon Sword combo! And with my Boosted Gear—"

"The Crimson-Haired Princess of Annihilation, the Vestal of Thunder, Sword Birth, and the Boosted Gear. Such grand-sounding names. But your opponent is the Phoenix. No matter what amazing powers you possess, you cannot defeat the immortal bird."

"Even a phoenix has its weaknesses!" I shot back.

Ravel snorted. "Are you going to keep beating him until he loses the will to fight? Or maybe you're planning to blast him with that God-class finishing move of yours? Do you really think you can win this match? Don't make me laugh!"

"What's wrong with that?!"

"From the very beginning, Lady Rias never stood a chance! All you can do is despair in the face of absolute immortality!" With that, Ravel clicked her fingers, and the remaining members of Riser's Familia circled around me.

"Karlamine!" Ravel called out next. "We'll leave the Knight to you. But if you lose, the rest of us won't stick to one-on-one combat. We'll take them down together. Or do you want to drag the name of the House of Phenex through the mud even more than you already have?"

Karlamine responded with a reluctant nod.

"Siris?"

"As you will." A wild-looking young woman stepped forward. She carried a large sword slung over her back.

"Siris is my brother's other Knight. Unlike Karlamine, she doesn't concern herself with all that chivalry nonsense. She crushes her enemies, and that's all there is to it."

This new Knight drew her sword from the sheath on her back... It was a huge weapon, and the blade was incredibly wide. A hit from that undoubtedly would've been fatal.

"But she can add the finishing touches. As for the rest... Ni? Li?"

"Meow?"

"Meow-meow?"

It was the two girls with animal ears who responded. They were Pawns, if I remembered correctly.

"These two are beast warriors. They specialize in martial arts."

Whoosh!

The cat-eared girls vanished from sight. The next moment, two powerful blows dug into my abdomen and face!

"Guh!"

I didn't even have time to cry out in pain as they laid into my entire body.

They moved so fast, I couldn't even tell where their fists were!

"B-Boosted Gear!"

"Boost!"

I started doubling my power, but my new opponents' attacks only grew stronger.

"Ni! Li! The Boosted Gear doubles the strength of his abilities every ten seconds! If you let him double it three times, he'll beat you just like he beat the chain-saw twins, Ile and Nel! You have to finish him within twenty seconds! He can't fight while he's boosting; all he'll be able to do is run! Aim for his legs! Be careful he doesn't touch you with his hand, too! Otherwise he'll use that disgusting technique of his to strip off your clothes!"

At this explanation, the two beast girls flashed me looks of fear and disgust.

"You're the worst!"

"Freak!"

Shut up! What's the problem?! What's wrong with mastering a move that strips girls naked?!

"All you do is think with your loins!" one of them said.

"And what's wrong with that?! I'm a guy!" I replied, knowing that answering was likely pointless.

It'd been surprising to learn that Ravel had discerned my weaknesses so quickly.

Gah! Ow! Damn it! They had gone straight for my legs! A low kick collided with my thighs.

Who would have thought that a beast girl could've kicked so ferociously? I wondered if perhaps their basic stats were higher than those of normal people.

Countering recklessly while the Boosted Gear was still charging wasn't an option. Starting from zero would've made me a sitting duck. I had to run.

Bam!

"Augh!" Another low kick! It certainly was effective. The pain shooting through my legs kept me rooted in place.

"Gah!" Next was a heavy punch that dug into my face. My eyes caught a streak of blood that had come from my nose and mouth. I could feel the tears welling in my eyes from the sheer pain!

"Issei! Damn it!"

Kiba, realizing my situation, quickly adjusted his hold on his sword, positioning himself to finish Karlamine in a hurry.

"Karlamine! Keep him busy for another ten seconds! I know you can't beat their Knight, but we only need a little longer to bury their Dragon User! Just keep him tied down until we're done!" Riser's sister called out with an ecstatic laugh.

Damn her, watching from on high! She was seriously getting on my nerves!

Thud!

My legs wouldn't move anymore. I fell to my knees. It was no good. There was no strength left in my limbs, and my mind was starting to feel groggy. I'd been beaten down too much.

Shit! I cursed myself. *If I pass out, I'll be retired!* I couldn't let that happen. There was no way I was going to drop out before even helping Rias!

Booooom!

A powerful tremor shook the battlefield. On the roof of the new school building, Rias and Riser were launching attack after attack at each other. Rias's crimson powers and Riser's fiery strikes were colliding in midair.

Riser appeared unharmed. His clothes didn't even look scuffed. Rias's, on the other hand, were torn in a number of places. Her breathing was growing ragged, too.

"*From the very beginning, Lady Rias never stood a chance! All you can do is despair in the face of absolute immortality!*" Ravel's words echoed in my mind.

Are we really about to lose? Is Rias? What's going to happen? Will Rias have to...with him...?

I couldn't let that happen! I had to find a way to get back on my feet. I had to stand, even if it meant getting beaten to a pulp.

Why did I want to keep fighting, though? Because I liked her? That was part of it. Love was my weakness. More than that, however, I wanted to protect the prez.

It didn't have anything to do with pacts or promises.

She had to remain the grand, majestic person I most longed for. The one who ran a hand through her brilliant crimson hair.

So give me your strength, Red Dragon Emperor!

The prez was the person I most admired. Rias had said that she didn't want to marry Riser. She had told me to fight. Which was why I *had to* fight.

Hey, Red Dragon Emperor! If you're listening, answer me!

"Give me your strength, Boosted Gear!"

"*Dragon Booster!*"

My Sacred Gear flashed with crimson light.

But it wasn't enough. It still wasn't enough. I needed more!

"More! Last time, it was for Asia! Now I need it for Rias! Show me what you've got! Boosted Gear!"

"Dragon Booster: Second Liberation!"

A voice I'd never heard before sounded from the gauntlet, and as it did so, a red aura enveloped my arm. All at once, the gauntlet began to transform.

"...Whoa? It changed again?"

......

The gauntlet, a crystallization of extraordinary power, had gained a new form. In addition to the gemstone embedded in the area covering the back of my hand, another had appeared on my arm, and the overall shape of the object had changed ever so slightly.

What's happening? No sooner had the thought crossed my mind, however, than fresh knowledge flowed into it.

So that's how I use this new power... I found my lips curling in a grin.

In that moment, I understand that I—no, *we*—could be stronger still!

"Kiba!"

Gathering my strength, I poured energy into my legs and shot up to my feet. I could feel my body screaming in agony, but I had to keep moving just a little more!

I started running toward Kiba.

"Use your Sacred Gear!" I cried out.

Kiba looked as if he didn't understand what I was saying, but he nonetheless plunged his sword into the ground and declared, "Sword Birth!"

Ching!

With a brilliant flash of light, countless Demon Swords burst forth from the ground. This was it!

I reached out to that burst of light and cried: "Boosted Gear: Second Power!"

I increased my energy with the Boosted Gear and directed it straight into the ground! My target was Kiba's Demon Sword creation ability!

"Boosted Gear Gift!"

"Transfer!"

Crash!

A metallic rumbling sound began to issue from all around. The entire athletic area had become a sea of swords. Blades of every shape imaginable jutted forth from the ground, reaching up to the sky. Everywhere I looked, there were countless more.

They had all been forged from Kiba's ability by way of my second power, Boosted Gear Gift, a bequest from the Red Dragon Emperor.

In effect, it allowed me to transfer my accumulated power to another person or object to increase their own potential. I'd channeled my power through the ground and into Kiba's Sacred Gear, and this was the result.

Kiba's weapon-creation skill had been elevated, and so the area around him was now riddled with new swords.

"...Impossible!"

"Is this another of the Dragon's powers...?"

The voices of Riser's servants were filled with anguish, and understandably so. They had all been skewered by the countless blades that had so suddenly erupted from the earth. Their bodies glowed with light as they disappeared from the field.

I had taken every one of them off the board!

"Two of Lord Riser's Pawns, two of his Knights, and one of his Bishops have been retired."

"Yes!"

As Grayfia's announcement echoed across the field, I adopted a proud victory pose.

One sudden move had taken them all down!

I can do this! We can do this! With this new Gift ability, I could boost not only Kiba's powers but Rias's and Akeno's, too. Even Asia's healing could be bolstered!

With this, there was no doubt in my mind that we were going to take Riser down!

"Issei... I'm impressed. That power..." Kiba glanced around at the new landscape. He looked to be taken aback by the efficacy of his own ability when pushed to overdrive.

"Yep. I used my gauntlet to boost your powers, Kiba."

At that moment, the last thing I'd been expecting to hear sounded in my ears: *"Lady Rias Gremory's Queen has been retired."*

"—?!"

"What?!"

Neither Kiba nor I could believe what we'd just heard! It was unbelievable! Akeno was the strongest of us all!

Booooom!

The ground shook violently as a familiar explosive sound reverberated. It had come from where Kiba was standing. Panicked, I glanced back toward him, only to freeze in place.

Kiba, our Knight, was lying flat on the ground, smoke rising up from his body.

The earth around him was covered in blood. Before I could even move to reach him, his body flashed with light and disappeared.

"Lady Rias Gremory's Knight has been retired," came yet another disheartening announcement.

I could only stand rooted to the ground in a mute daze at this incomprehensible turn of events.

With almost everyone on both sides out of the Rating Game, I was left standing alone on the athletic grounds.

Crack…!

Without Kiba, the Demon Swords littering the area around me began to shatter one by one.

The fragments of those blades glittered with silver light as they danced through the air, the whole scene giving everything a phantasmagorical atmosphere. After only a few seconds, all the weapons had faded away.

—!

Unfortunately, I didn't have time to grieve this new development. A shadow floated into my field of vision from overhead. When I looked up, I saw that it was a hooded mage: Riser's Queen!

She was supposed to have been fighting Akeno! Thoughts began to race through my mind. Had only Akeno been retired? This Queen didn't even look injured! What was going on? Akeno couldn't have lost!

"Another Knight crushed," Riser's Queen said with a derisive laugh.

At that moment, a wave of anger overtook me. "Are you the one who did in Akeno and Kiba?!"

The explosion had been the same kind that'd caught Koneko, and now this mage lady had taken Kiba, too?!

"Get down here! I'll tear you apart! For Akeno, for Koneko, and for Kiba! I'll beat you to a pulp; I'll kill you!" I pointed up into the air, trying to provoke the Queen. Even after such a threat, she merely broke into a scornful grin before losing interest and soaring off toward the roof of the new school building.

"Wait! Get back here!" Enraged, I took off after her. Like hell was I about to let her get away! The prez and Asia were up there! I refused to allow that damn Queen to hurt any more of my friends! I would kill her first!

Snap!

"Argh!"

My legs gave way, and I tumbled down to the ground. I tried to pull myself back up, but I had no strength left... My whole body was trembling uncontrollably...

The reason was obvious; I'd reached my limit.

It was only thanks to Rias's training that I had lasted so long, but this was the clear outcome for someone who lacked any real combat experience. My heart was racing painfully fast, and each breath was a chore. Everything ached so painfully that it was difficult to form thoughts.

My mental state wasn't particularly good, either. I had lost my friends right in front of my eyes. It wasn't particularly unusual to lose your mind after being exposed to one heartrending scene after another.

Still, I had to get up.

Even with the situation as grim as it was, my only concern was to standing back up and going to help Rias.

"Ngahhhhhhhhhhhhh!" I cried out at the top of my lungs, hoping to muster whatever strength I could. As long as I was still in the game, I had a chance! Slowly, I rose to my feet and turned toward the school building.

Okay, I just need to get up onto the roof now. That plan was quickly dashed, however, when a voice called out to me.

"Are you still raring to fight?"

I looked over my shoulder, only to see Riser's sister, Ravel, descending from above on her black wings.

Evidently, Kiba's Demon Swords had failed to take her down. Perhaps she'd dodged by flying high up into the air? As I thought about it, I realized that the announcement had said that only one of Riser's Bishops had been retired.

I readied myself, adopting a fighting posture, but Ravel merely shrugged.

"I'm not interested in fighting anymore," she said. "I mean, no matter how you look at it, you've already lost."

"Shut up. The prez is still standing, and so am I."

"That Dragon power is unnerving. To transfer your energy to someone else and boost their abilities…that's not normal. I shudder to think what would happen if you did that with the Vestal of Thunder or with Lady Rias. In future Rating Games, that ability may well pose a threat even to the greatest of opponents, but your team has lost this match."

"…Because the Phoenix is immortal?"

"That too, but the real reason is that neither you nor Lady Rias has any real fight left in you, right? Even if you can heal your wounds, that won't restore your strength. Look at you; you're all worn out. Defeat is inevitable. And besides—" Ravel paused there. She produced a container of something that looked like Holy Water. That should've been impossible, though.

"—Phoenix Tears. Have you heard of them? They can heal any wound."

Phoenix Tears?! Rias had mentioned them during our training camp. I'd never expected Riser's group to actually have any.

"Don't call us cheats, if that's what you're thinking. Your Familia has the Twilight Healing, no?" Ravel said, as if having read my mind. "Besides, the rules clearly state that Phoenix Tears can only be used by two demons in any one game. In today's case, our Queen and I are the ones with them. That's how Yubelluna defeated your Vestal of Thunder. They fetch a high price on the market, you know. Selling the tears has brought great prosperity to the House of Phenex. Yep, ever since the Rating Game came into fashion, we've been doing pretty well. Immortality and Phoenix Tears make us pretty tough to beat."

Ravel kept prattling on with one proud boast after another.

Phoenix Tears… If Riser's team could heal even in the midst of battle, then not even Akeno could've stood much of a chance… Wallowing in self-pity was unlikely to get me anywhere, however.

Steeling myself, I continued forward.

"H-hey! Hold up! Are you ignoring me?! You're going to lose anyway, so you're better off staying here and chatting with me, don't you think?!"

"Shut up. Talk to yourself, chicken girl. Come any closer and I'll strip you naked."

Ravel retreated a half step, reflexively shielding her body. It was the exact sort of response I'd been expecting.

I took off toward the school building with Ravel's shrill voice at my back.

Entering the building through the back entrance, I headed down the corridors. My destination was the rooftop—and Rias!

Thump.

Something pulsated through me. I could feel my attributes changing. I had entered enemy territory, which meant that I had satisfied the necessary conditions!

"Promotion: Queen!"

Power welled up inside me. I took off down the corridor, but...

"Aughhhhh!"

Violently, I collapsed to the floor. All the feeling in my legs was gone. It was a telltale sign that I'd surpassed the limits of my physical endurance. Even though I'd increased my abilities, I had zero energy left to actually use them.

A little thing like that wasn't going to stop me, though! I was going to crawl to the rooftop if I had to!

Akeno was gone. Koneko was gone. Kiba was gone.

Each of my allies had been defeated. I was the only one left capable of protecting Rias! What good was I if I couldn't even keep moving?!

I won't lose! I won't allow it! Prez! I'll give you this victory! Just you watch!

Once again, I rose, only to come crashing down again and again... So long as I could move forward with each fall, I was still going to reach my destination.

My face and body were slick with sweat, blood, tears, and saliva, but I was almost there...

At last, the door to the rooftop came into view! Without pausing to catch my breath, I forced it open.

—!

There in front of me, Rias and Riser were still going at it. Asia was watching on helplessly from a distance. It was reassuring to see that they both were still okay.

That said, Rias wasn't exactly having an easy time. Her beautiful crimson hair was in disarray, and her clothes were in tatters.

I took a deep breath, then bellowed, "Prez! Issei Hyoudou, reporting for duty!" Everyone's gazes turned in my direction.

"Issei!" Rias and Asia cried back in unison.

At last, I'd made it! I didn't have to keep them waiting any longer!

"The Dragon brat? Ravel let him go, did she?" Riser clicked his tongue in irritation.

Perhaps his younger sister was going through some kind of rebellious phase. It was only because she hadn't tried to stop me that I'd made it this far.

At that moment, Riser's Queen alighted from above to stand next to him. "Master Riser, shall I take care of the Pawn boy and Lady Rias's dear little Bishop? You should know, he possesses a rather awkward ability. He can strip his opponent's clothes right off."

The Queen took a step in my direction, but Riser held out his hand to keep her back. "Are you worried he might extinguish the flames that protect my body? I wonder. Taking his personality into consideration, I have a feeling his technique will only work on ladies. I will face Rias and her servants myself. That's the only way to settle this, wouldn't you say?"

What's with that self-confident attitude of his? Is he trying to give us some kind of last stand because he's sure he'll win?

Riser hadn't been wrong about my Dress Break ability, though. Indeed, it was effective only on the feminine form. That was how I'd created this ability, by imagining the naked bodies of women. I didn't want to see a naked guy, let alone touch one!

I'd used it to peel fruit and vegetables, but I still had my doubts it would work on a man.

"Quit messing around, Riser!" Rias cried out with indignation as she hurled a ball of demonic energy straight for his face.

He didn't even try to dodge it.

Whoa, it blew half his head off! Rias did it! At least, that's what I'd thought. A wave of red-hot flames erupted from the gaping wound. The fire coalesced into the shape of Riser's head, and when it

subsided, his face was whole again. Riser stretched his neck as if nothing had happened.

Immortality... So this is the regeneration ability of the Phoenix.

"Give up, Rias. This continued resistance of yours doesn't reflect
well on your father or Lord Sirzechs. You're out of options. We all
know how this is going to play out. It's checkmate." Riser spoke as if
admonishing her.

Unfazed, Rias glared back. "Be quiet, Riser. I won't give up! You
know how this is going to end? You think I have no more options?
Well, I'm sorry to disappoint, but this King is still raring to go!" she
said with a dauntless grin.

I was getting pretty pumped up, too. So long as Rias was still had
some fight in her, this wasn't over! Trusting that we were going to turn
this around somehow, I ran toward Rias, inserting myself between her
and Riser.

"Asia!" I called out.

At this, Asia glanced timidly at Riser and his Queen before
approaching to join me.

Neither Riser nor Yubelluna made any move to come after either of
us. That's not to say I'd expected them to, but they were clearly both
getting a little too overconfident!

Asia began to heal Rias's injuries and then attended to mine. As her
hand touched our bodies, a warm, pale-green light enveloped us.

She washed away my pain, leaving my body feeling as if the agony
I'd been enduring was nothing but a bad dream. My swollen face
returned to normal, and the numbness in my legs faded.

Unfortunately, Asia's healing did nothing for exhaustion. I was
going to have to do something about my lack of stamina...

"Asia! Once you've finished healing me, get down."

"—!" Asia looked startled. Judging by her shocked expression, she
clearly hadn't been expecting me to say that.

"You need to stay back so that you can heal the prez and me. You're
our lifeline."

There was a pained look on Asia's face, as if she'd wanted to say something. The blond girl kept quiet and took a step back, however.

That's fine, I thought. *So long as she's safe—*

"Argh!" A sudden scream burst from Asia's lips.

What?! A magic circle I'd never seen before had appeared beneath her feet. It seemed to be preventing her from moving.

"Sorry about that," Riser said indifferently. "I would feel bad dragging this out for you. I could have just defeated her...but all I needed to do was stop her from being able to heal you. That magic circle will only be released if you can take down my Queen."

I glanced at Yubelluna. She was holding out her hand, and her fingertips were glowing.

Damn her! Asia was our last hope!

There was no use complaining now; the last battle was about to begin.

"Prez. We're still going to do this, right?"

"Yeah!"

Judging by Rias's voice, she hadn't given up yet! We still had a chance!

"You, Asia, and I are the only ones left. But Asia's trapped, and he's immortal. Not to mention, there are still two members of his Familia standing. The odds don't look good," I said in a loud voice with a fearless smile. "But I won't surrender. I don't know much about how these things usually play out, and I don't much care for our options. All I'm going to do is fight. I'll keep fighting until the very end!"

"Well said, Issei! Let's take Riser down together!" Rias said proudly.

"Of course, Prez!"

You hear that, Boosted Gear? My master gave me an order! This should be pretty easy, right? All I've got to do is beat that guy into submission. That's all there is to it.

"Let's go!"

"*Burst!*"

How I wished I hadn't heard that sound.

As soon as that word emanated from the gemstone on the back of my gauntlet, my body felt suddenly heavy, and then it seemingly stopped functioning entirely. I could feel myself losing consciousness.

No! Not yet!

I crawled on all fours, coughing up a mouthful of something bitter and metallic.

It was blood.

My body had been pushed well past what it was capable of.

The light on the back of my gauntlet faded away. I, its user, was no longer capable of functioning.

I'd just been healed, though. I should've still been able to fight...

Riser stared down at me. "The Boosted Gear exhausts its user more than you can imagine. Continuously doubling your power is too extreme. The burden it places on your body goes beyond any regular Sacred Gear. Running around this battlefield, fighting my servants one after the next—you hit your maximum a long time ago."

No, I thought. *No matter what that bastard says, I'm not done.*

Rias looked at me with sorrow in her eyes, and I felt a pang of guilt.

This is no problem. I can stand.

With no small amount of difficulty I channeled every fiber of my being into dragging myself to my feet. How many times had I pulled myself back from the brink of death now?

"Let's go, Prez!"

With that last declaration, I took off toward Riser.

"Gah!"

An intense pain gripped my body.

I'd long since lost count of how many times such a sensation had surged through me today. Over and over, I'd crumbled to the ground and made a total ass of myself.

Prez... Let's win this. I can still fight.

Rias was already on her knees, no longer able to stand. She had used all her powers. She had attacked Riser countless times, inflicted more injuries on him than could be counted, but no matter what she did, he merely healed afterward with a flash of fire, as if nothing had ever happened.

I needed to protect her, and Asia, too… I was the only one left who could…

Wham!

Riser pummeled his fist straight into my stomach, twisting and grinding his knuckles into my abdomen.

Gah!

Blood gushed from my mouth… I had already vomited up so much, but apparently, I still had more in me.

My vision was becoming blurry… I shook my head, trying to restore my fading sight.

I'm okay… I can win… I'll beat Riser… This is my present to Rias… Something like that would make her smile, right? I swear to make both her and Asia happy… Thank you, Prez, for all that time you spent training me… It's thanks to you that I'm still standing. I might be only a Pawn, but I'll be the mightiest Pawn of all time!

Slam!

This time, Riser's fist dug deep into my face. The moment he hit me, everything seemed to start moving in slow motion.

Prez… I can keep going.

I have…to keep…my promise…

…I would win for her…

Checkmate

It was over.

I—Rias Gremory—was out of options. In other words, it was checkmate.

None of us had any strength left to fight.

Even so, he had still come for me. He alone had risen to continue fighting at my side.

Issei.

He was the only one who'd kept pushing on, who'd challenged Riser in the face of certain defeat.

All that effort had been for nothing, though. Riser's last strike had finished him.

Watching Issei fall numbly backward, I found myself running toward him and taking him in my arms.

He was covered in blood and sweat. To be honest, he looked terrible, and yet, I loved him still.

"...Issei, you fought well. You've done enough. You did everything you could," I whispered to him gently, but he continued to try to pull himself back to his feet.

"That's enough, Issei!" I cried, but still he pushed my hands away. For what must have been the hundredth time, Issei forced himself back upright.

In wordless silence, he took one step forward and then another.

My heart cried out at his unrelenting intensity of spirit. Everyone around us watched on with bated breath. His foe, Riser, approached him expressionlessly.

No! If this kept up, I would lose him forever.

My cute little servant. My Issei. No matter what happened here, I was still going to adore him, to coddle him. I couldn't lose him in a place like this! Pacing forward, I put myself between him and Riser, holding Issei by his shoulders.

"Issei! Stop! Can't you hear me?" But I fell silent at what I saw.

Of course. He... He... Issei...

Issei had already lost consciousness.

His eyes were vacant, and his mouth hung slack, but somehow he kept pushing himself forward, step by grueling step.

His clenched fists wouldn't stop shaking...

"...Even now, you're still fighting for me..."

Before I knew it, tears were running down my cheeks. I reached out to touch his face.

It was swollen, and I could sense nothing of the vigorous spirit that usually resided inside him.

"...Silly Issei."

Though he was still trying to move forward, I wrapped my arms around him.

"You've done enough."

With those words, his strength finally left his body, and he fell to the ground in my arms.

I held him close, laying him on my lap. I had promised him another lap pillow, after all.

He had fought for me.

"Prez! I'll give you this victory! Just you watch!"

He didn't even know how to properly make use of his demonic powers yet, but he'd still pushed onward across the battlefield with all his heart. He'd hardly even had any fighting experience.

That boy should've been terrified. He could've lost his life countless times over...

"I won't surrender. I don't know much about how these things usually play out, and I don't much care for our options. All I'm going to do is fight. I'll keep fighting until the very end!"

He was so battered and bruised, his fists so badly swollen, and still he was fighting for me...

Issei was someone who was always smiling. He was always pouring his heart and soul into everything and was always doing his absolute best for me.

Standing there on that rooftop, I thought I was about to lose that smile of his forever.

"Thank you, Akeno, Yuuto, Koneko, Asia...and Issei. Thank you for fighting so hard for someone as worthless as me."

I softly stroked Issei's head once more before turning to Riser.

"You win. I concede."

It was my first Rating Game. My career had started with a bitter, grueling defeat.

I knew I was never going to forget what had happened that day.

Endgame

Red. I had a dream of red.

An entity inside me suddenly scolded me. It was telling me that the power I'd been wielding wasn't my true strength.

Who is it? I wondered. *The Sacred Gear? Something else lurking within me?*

Its lips curled upward with a flicker of incandescent flame.

"You'll never grow stronger like that."

An unknown voice echoed in my mind.

The thing was more than just my imagination. It had come from somewhere deep inside me. Had it been my heart? No… It was my left arm.

"You're an exceptional being, a vessel of a Dragon. Don't make such a miserable sight of yourself again. Do you want the White One to laugh at you?"

"Are you that Dragon who appeared in my dream? Was it you who gave me that new power-up?" I asked.

"Indeed. That was what you desired, what I desired, and what the White One desired. So you managed to reach a new level."

"'*Desired*'…? What are you talking about? And just who is this 'White One'?!"

"You will meet him one of these days. He and I are destined to do battle. Speaking of which, allow me to teach you how to use my true power."

I had no idea what the voice was talking about.

"Just who—?"

"I am the Red Dragon Emperor, the Welsh Dragon Ddraig. I reside in your left arm, Issei Hyoudou."

"The Welsh Dragon…Ddraig…?"

"*Losing is fine. So long as you're alive, defeat can add to your strength. But it is only worthwhile if you can win the next time. Defeat followed by victory followed by yet more victory. If you can do that, you will meet him one day.*"

"What exactly is happening to me?"

"*You'll understand soon enough. In the meantime, continue to develop your strength. I will grant you my power whenever you need it. What I give comes at a cost, but it will be worth the sacrifice. Use it to strike back at those who belittle you. That is what it means to be a Dragon.*"

Life.∞ vs. Power.∞
I'm Here to Keep My Promise!

A familiar sight greeted me when I opened my eyes.

It was the ceiling of my bedroom.

What am I doing here?

Desperately, I pored through my muddled memories. I was supposed to be in the middle of a Rating Game match between the prez and Riser. The battlefield had been a replica of Kuou Academy.

The old school building had been our headquarters, and I'd been in the middle of an assault against the enemy team's headquarters in the new school building along with Kiba and Koneko.

Koneko had fallen first, followed by Akeno and Kiba, and then—

It all came flooding back to me.

What happened to Rias?! What about the match?! How did it end?! Did we beat Riser?! Why am I here?!

I sat straight up in my bed.

"You're awake," came a woman's voice beside me.

It was the silver-haired maid Grayfia.

"Grayfia! What happened? Is Rias all right?!"

"Lord Riser won the match. Lady Rias resigned."

—! *Th-that's...* I was speechless. No words could've described how I was feeling.

So Riser really beat me? I felt like a disgrace.

I had acted so high-and-mighty, but when it came down to it, I'd let myself get beaten to a pulp in front of Rias.

Why am I so weak? Asia would've been able to live a normal life if not for my complete and utter uselessness. Maybe if I'd made better use of my Sacred Gear, Rias wouldn't have ended up having to...

I couldn't stop myself from crying. Even with Grayfia sitting next to me, I was bawling openly. I was disgusted with myself.

"Lord Riser's and Lady Rias's engagement party is taking place as we speak. It is being held at a venue chosen by the House of Gremory in the demon realm."

"...What about Kiba and the others?"

"They are escorting Lady Rias. The only members of her Familia not in attendance are yourself and Miss Asia."

Asia? She isn't going, either?

"Lady Rias asked that she remain here to take care of you, Master Issei. She is currently downstairs fetching a fresh towel for you."

Evidently, the prez had assigned Asia to watch over me. The little nun must've been pretty worried for me.

Prez... Engagement... They're in the middle of the celebration?

"...Am I correct in assuming you won't accept this situation?" Grayfia asked.

"Yeah. Even with how the match ended, I can't just let this happen."

"You understand that Lady Rias is acting in accordance with her family's wishes?"

"Of course I know that! But still, I..."

No matter how I tried, I couldn't get myself to agree to something I knew Rias was so opposed to. I didn't want to see her marrying that bastard against her will just because her parents had told her to. There was no way I was going to let Riser have Rias!

I knew what this was: jealousy. I was overwhelmed with feelings of envy for that damn roast chicken. Giving Rias to someone like him went against everything I stood for.

At that moment, Grayfia let out a gentle chuckle. It was my first time seeing her smile. Previously, she'd always seemed so distant and composed.

"You're an interesting one. I've met a great many demons over the years, but I've never seen someone as fervently dedicated to their beliefs as you. My master, Lord Sirzechs, was watching your performance during the match. He was quite impressed."

Seriously? I had impressed one of the Demon Kings? Hearing that Rias's brother, the Demon King Lucifer, had taken such an interest in me left me at a loss as to how best to reply.

Grayfia reached into her pocket and produced a piece of paper with a magic circle printed on it.

"This will take you straight to the venue of the engagement party."

—! Wh-why does she have something like that?!

"Lord Sirzechs has a message for you." Grayfia paused for a second, and her expression turned dire. *"'If you wish to save my sister, force your way into that hall.'* Those were his words. There is another magic circle on the other side of that paper. Use it once you have located Lady Rias. I'm sure you'll find it helpful."

No words were coming to me. Grayfia placed the card in my hand and rose to leave.

"I sensed tremendous power lurking inside you while you were sleeping, Master Issei. A Dragon is the only kind of being associated not with God, nor with demons, nor with the fallen angels. If that terrible power lurks within you..." Her words trailed off there, and she left the room.

I was alone... But there was nothing that needed thinking over.

I got out of bed and rummaged around for something to wear, only to find a brand-new uniform folded up neatly on my desk.

My last one had been torn to shreds during the battle. Had someone prepared a fresh one? Grayfia? Rias? Whoever it was, I was grateful.

I quickly put on my clothes, then grabbed the scrap with the magic circles on it.

At that moment, my bedroom door swung open, and Asia entered the room.

"Issei!"

The moment she saw me, the towel and the bucket of water she had been holding in her hands fell to the floor. Immediately after that, she jumped right into my arms.

Whoa. Asia, what's wrong? Having her come at me like that so suddenly was pretty embarrassing.

"I'm so glad you're all right. Your wounds were so severe that you didn't wake up for more than two days... I was worried you might never open your eyes again... Issei..."

Still holding on to me tightly, she began to weep. I'd made her cry again. I patted her softly on the head, trying to get her to relax.

Hold on. I've been asleep for two whole days...? It's been that long since the match? What have I been doing this whole time?! I can't afford to slack off at a time like this!

"Asia, listen to me. I'm going to find the prez."

"—!"

Asia was clearly shocked by what I'd said. She no doubt suspected what I planned to do.

"...You're not going...to join the celebrations...are you...?"

"No. I'm going to bring her back. Don't worry. I have a way of getting there."

"I'm going, too!" she said without a moment's hesitation. Her expression was grave. She meant it.

"You can't. I need you to stay here."

"No! I can fight with you, Issei! I've learned how to use my powers! I'm sick of just having others take care of me! I need to give something in return!"

Asia grabbed my hands.

It almost sounded like she was saying that she didn't want to leave my side, but I knew that couldn't have been it.

"No. You need to stay here. I'll bring her back. See, this is the kind of thing the Boosted Gear was made for. Don't worry—it'll be all right. I'll beat Riser to a pulp, and then—"

"It won't be all right!" Asia cried.

Tears streamed down from her beautiful green eyes.

"...You'll get hurt again... Bloody, broken... All that pain... I don't want you to suffer again, Issei..."

I had been badly injured in my fight with the fallen angel back when I'd gone to rescue her from that group of exorcists, and the same had happened during my last fight with Riser.

Both times, I would've probably died if Asia hadn't healed me.

I could vividly remember her crying over my body as she treated my wounds. No doubt I was going to give her further cause to weep in the days and weeks to come.

That much was fairly clear.

Putting on a wide smile, I took her hand in mine. "I'm not going to die. I promise. I didn't die when I went to save you, did I? That's why I'll be okay. I'll live, and I'll come back to you, and we'll have so many more good times together."

Wiping away her tears, Asia gave me a slight nod. "...In that case, make me another promise, too."

"Another promise?"

"Make sure you bring the president back with you," she said with a warm smile.

"Ah, of course," I answered.

At this, Asia's expression deepened into one of pure joy.

Right. I remembered there was something I had to tell her. "Asia, actually..."

Once I had explained the situation to her, she immediately nodded in agreement and went to her room to fetch what I needed.

That done, the only thing left to do now was... I closed my eyes and addressed the entity that resided inside me: *Hey, if you're listening, come out! You're there, aren't you? Welsh Dragon Ddraig, we need to talk! Come out already!*

Not long after I summoned him, an eerie voice broke into laughter from somewhere inside me. *"What is it, kid? What do you need?"*

—○●○—

Whoosh...

Using the magic circle Grayfia had given me, I jumped to a strange and unfamiliar place. I'd been afraid that I wouldn't be able to warp properly because of my paltry powers, but there'd been something unique about the circle on that piece of paper.

Glancing around, I saw that I was in a seemingly endless corridor. Candle-like objects lined the walls, and in between them were portraits of stately red-haired men. Relatives of Rias, perhaps?

There was no time to dawdle. I could make out the sound of distant voices down the hall, and so I set out in that direction.

Before long, I came across a huge, open doorway. There was some kind of intricate engraving on it. Upon closer inspection, it appeared to be a sort of demonic beast. I couldn't concern myself with that at the moment, however.

Inside the hall, a great crowd of well-dressed demons was busy chatting and laughing with one another. It looked no different than the kind of event that high-class human social circles often held. Not that I had ever been to one. But it fit my mental image like a glove.

I scanned the faces in the crowd, looking to find one I recognized.

The hall was gargantuan. It had to have been larger than even the grounds of my school. The ceiling was imperceptibly high, and there was an incredibly ornate, gigantic chandelier illuminating the room.

So this is the venue organized by Rias's family? I thought. It must have been nice to be as wealthy as they clearly were. I couldn't wait to get a peerage of my own and make a name for myself in this demon world.

While lost in such thoughts, I noticed a burst of crimson from the corner of my eye.

A woman, with her brilliant crimson hair tied up in an elegant coiffure. She was wearing a red dress. I recognized her at once. How could I have not?

"Prez!"

Before I knew it, I had called out to her from across the hall.

Everyone around me turned in my direction, as did Rias herself.

There was no mistaking the sight of her eyes opening wide in surprise as a solitary tear ran down her cheek.

Silently, she mouthed my name.

That bastard Riser was standing next to her in a garish tuxedo. What did he think he was doing showing off in an outfit like that?!

I took a deep breath before declaring: "All high-class demons here! And Rias's brother, Lord Demon King! I am Issei Hyoudou of the Occult Research Club at Kuou Academy! And I'm taking the prez, Rias Gremory, home!"

The hall broke out into hushed murmurs.

Paying them no heed, I stormed toward Rias and Riser.

"Hey, you! What do you think you're—?"

I had caught the attention of someone who looked like a security guard. But then three more figures appeared to intercept him.

"Issei! Leave this to us!" Kiba said, dressed in a white tuxedo.

"...You're late." Koneko, her petite build garbed in an elegant dress, appeared next to him.

"Oh dear. So you finally showed up?" Lastly there was Akeno, wearing an extravagant kimono.

The three of them moved to intercept the guards who were coming my way.

"Thanks," I murmured as I approached Riser.

Standing boldly before that jackass, I bluntly announced, "Rias Gremory's virginity belongs to me!"

"!!!"

Riser's eyes twitched in a way that belied all description.

"What's going on, Riser?"

"Lady Rias? What's the meaning of this?"

The relatives and acquaintances of both families appeared genuinely confused by this turn of events. It looked like high-class demons were no different than humans when it came to dealing with sudden surprises.

"This is my doing."

At that moment, a red-haired man stepped forward. He was one of the figures whose portrait I had seen in the corridor. His features were remarkably close to Rias's...

"Brother," Rias said.

Hold on. This is her brother?! I-i-in that case... H-h-he's the D-D-Demon King Sirzechs Lucifer?!

"I wanted to see the power of a Dragon for myself, so I had Grayfia help him."

"L-Lord Sirzechs! Y-you can't just...!" Some middle-aged man, probably a relative of Rias and Sirzechs, was becoming incredibly flustered.

"What's the problem? I enjoyed watching the Rating Game. Although I couldn't help but feel a little bad for my younger sister. She was facing off against the mighty Riser, scion of the great Phenex family, while she herself was completely lacking in combat experience."

"...Lord Sirzechs, are you suggesting the match was unfair?"

"No, not at all. If I was to say something like that, these two great Houses would lose face. We must treasure the relations between high-class demon families, after all," Sirzechs answered with a shrewd smile.

Judging from what he was saying, it sounded like he was taking Rias's side.

"Then what do you suggest, Lord Sirzechs?" asked the man with the same crimson hair...

Crimson hair... Is he Rias's father?!

"Father. May I propose we make my dear sister's engagement party into a livelier affair? A Dragon versus a Phoenix. Wouldn't that be a contest to behold? Two legendary creatures to lighten the mood. Could there be any greater entertainment?"

At this suggestion, everyone in the hall fell silent.

Sirzechs turned toward me. "Wielder of a Dragon. You have my permission. Won't you show us your power once more, in the presence of Riser, Rias, and myself?"

Hearing this request, Riser broke out into a dauntless grin. "Why not? I can't refuse Lord Sirzechs, can I? Then this shall be my final performance before settling down for married life!"

...*Overconfident bastard*, I cursed. Still, with this, the stage was set. The only thing left was for me to emerge the victor!

Surprisingly, the Demon King had another question for me, however. "Wielder of the Dragon, what would you ask should you win?"

"Lord Sirzechs?!"

"What are you saying?!"

The gathered demons all balked at Sirzechs's question, their voices panicked.

Nonetheless, the Demon King paid no heed to the concerns of those around him. "He is a demon, after all. If we are going to ask him to do something for us, we must be willing to offer him something in return, wouldn't you say? So tell us. You can have anything you desire. A noble title of your own? The greatest beauty of the ages to live by your side?"

—*!*

What an incredible offer! He was willing to give me everything I had ever dreamed of. A place in the nobility! A beautiful woman! With just one word, I could've had it all! I'd already decided what to ask for, though.

"Please let me take Rias Gremory back with me," I answered without the slightest hesitation.

At this, the Demon King flashed me a truly satisfied smile. "Very well. Should you win, you may take her with you."

Thus, it was decided that Riser and I would face off in that very venue.

"Thank you!" I said with a bow of my head as Sirzechs disappeared toward the back of the hall.

The guests cleared a space in the center of the room before gathering around to watch on with keen interest.

Kiba, Koneko, and Akeno seated themselves with Rias and her family. Sirzechs, too, took a seat beside her.

On the other side sat the members of the House of Phenex, their relatives, and their servants. Riser's sister, Ravel, was among them.

Riser and I stood across from each other in the center of the hall. Judging by the layout, this must have been a demon-fighting ring at one point.

I had already activated my Boosted Gear.

Riser's expression was one of relaxed confidence.

"You may begin!" announced the male demon who had been selected to oversee the duel.

This was it! There was really no turning back now! The only option for me was to win!

Riser, his fiery wings spread, pointed toward my gauntlet. "I already know about all your tricks. The Gauntlet of the Red Dragon Emperor is a Sacred Gear that continuously doubles its user's strength and power, that's all. I've heard that you've developed a new technique for transferring that power to another, but it won't do you any good now."

It sounded like he knew about my new Boosted Gear Gift move, but I'd already guessed as much. That Gift technique was all the stronger when channeled through one of my allies.

I glanced toward Rias, flashing her a determined grin. "Prez, I'll settle this within ten seconds."

"...Issei?" She raised a quizzical eyebrow.

It's all right, Prez, I thought. *Just watch.*

"Ten seconds? You talk big. In that case, I'll finish you off in *five*. I won't hold back this time, Pawn!"

Riser Phenex! I'm going to crush you with everything I have!

"Prez! Let me use a Promotion here!" I called out.

Rias nodded.

Thump.

There was a ringing in my chest. That was all I needed to know that she had given me permission to use it.

"Promotion: Queen!"

With that, I was now the strongest piece! I could feel the power flowing through my body! I was at my climax right from the start of the match! There was just one more thing to do.

It's your turn, Red Dragon Emperor!

"Prez!" I called out to Rias. "I may not be a talented swordsman like Kiba! Or an expert at using my demonic powers like Akeno! I might not have Koneko's superhuman strength or Asia's healing ability! But I *will* be the mightiest of Pawns!" That much I knew I could swear.

"I'll take down God for you if I have to! With this Boosted Gear, my only weapon, I'll protect you!"

I'll protect her… I'm going to get stronger alongside my friends and allies!

"Burst! Overboost!"

"Welsh Dragon: Overbooster!"

The jewel embedded in the back of the gauntlet released a brilliant flash of red.

That red light illuminated the entire hall, and a deep crimson aura enveloped me.

Instantly, a deluge of overwhelming power flooded my body!

"Yeah, use it well. But only for ten seconds. Your body won't endure any more than that."

Got it! That'll be more than enough!

"Indeed. With ten seconds—"

Yep, with ten seconds—

"We'll pulverize him!"

With a brilliant burst of red light, I lunged forward.

A scarlet suit of armor appeared around me. It was a full-body set modeled after the image of a Dragon. It had a sharp, visceral appearance. A mirror of the gauntlet that I always wore on my left arm had appeared over my right one.

Additional jewels like the one embedded in the back of the gauntlet were visible on my arms, shoulders, knees, and chest.

Not only that, there was also a propulsion device like a rocket booster built into the back of the suit.

"Armor?! You've used the power of the Red Dragon Emperor to shield yourself?!" Riser exclaimed in surprise.

His assessment was on the mark.

I probably did look like a miniature Dragon. Even my face was concealed behind a plated helm.

"This is the power of the Red Dragon Emperor! Balance Breaker, Boosted Gear: Scale Mail! If you want to stop me, ask Lord Demon King! It sounds like this is a famous, dreaded, and forbidden technique!"

The Scale Mail ability released all the Sacred Gear's destructive potential in a ten-second burst.

Once it was activated, I was practically invincible. Unfortunately, it also carried considerable risk. Each time the ability was used, it rendered my Sacred Gear unusable for three whole days. The Red Dragon—Ddraig—had explained that to me. Basically, this was an all-or-nothing maneuver.

X

The countdown had begun. Now that it had started, there was no time to waste!

Let's settle this in one go, Riser Phenex!

I brought my hands close together, leaving only a slight gap between them, and summoned a tremendous mass of demonic energy.

Then, without any delay, I launched it straight for him.

That ball of raw power grew to a tremendous size as it sped toward Riser.

The strength of that blast was truly unbelievable. It must have been large enough to fill at least half the hall. Even I was taken aback!

"Damn, that's huge!"

Riser must not have been anticipating an attack of such magnitude, as he chose to leap to safety rather than meet it head-on. That was just the chance I needed.

IX

The clock was ticking. I had to hurry!

I threw myself in the direction that I expected Riser to run. The flight unit embedded in the back of my suit of armor burst to life. In less than an instant, I was accelerating at an explosive speed!

I couldn't so much as move my body due to the immense g-forces, but I was closing the distance to my target at an insane rate.

Riser, stunned, made no move to brace himself or respond.

It is time to attack! At least, that's what I'd thought. I still couldn't move, however.

Crash!

I slammed straight into the wall. What a mess! That had been the perfect opportunity, too!

I managed to raise my arms to protect myself before making impact, so I took no real damage. There was, however, a gaping crater in the wall leading to whatever lay outside.

Incredible! That was a huge crash, but the armor's totally fine!

Realizing how durable the suit was, I wondered if perhaps I could collide with my opponent without hurting myself.

VIII

There were only eight seconds left!

I rose to my feet, brushed off the fragments of the wall that were stuck to me, and turned back to Riser.

After that last attack, he was more on guard this time.

A rainbow aura encircled Riser. The tremendous energy raging around him made my skin crawl.

"You Red Dragon punk! You've done it now! I didn't want to say this, but you're nothing more than an animal! A freak! I'll kill you in front of your beloved master, Rias!" Riser roared, his wings of pure flame enlarging with explosive force.

Fire whirled around him, bathing the hall in scathing heat.

Onlookers conjured barriers to shield themselves. If those flames had come into contact with the guests, they likely would've been reduced to ash.

"I am of the House of Phenex! The flame of the immortal firebird burns within me! I will reduce you to dust!"

Riser, his whole body wrapped in a blistering mass of roiling flames, charged toward me.

That silhouette of flame morphed into the shape of a gigantic bird.

Its wings were born of unrivaled fire. Letting them touch me was clearly a bad idea.

"The flames of the immortal Phoenix can damage even my Dragon mail. You don't want to take too many hits from him."

Thanks for the heads-up, Ddraig.

Unfortunately, I had to meet Riser with everything I had. Rias was watching.

There's no other choice!

"What makes you think some pathetic embers are going to beat me?!" I cried out as I charged toward my opponent. The flight unit on my back propelled me forward at immense speed!

Slam!

As our fists struck each other's faces, the entire hall shuddered with the force of the shock wave. There, in the center of the venue, we began laying into each other with one strike after the next.

Ngh! Every time Riser hit me, the force of the impact reverberated through my body!

The heat was almost unbearable. Believe me when I say it was hot as hell! If not for my armor, the flames winding around that bastard's fists would've probably charred me to the bone—or worse!

I was scared. I wanted nothing more than to flee to safety! I didn't want to die! And the more we traded blows, the greater I sensed the difference in ability between us.

The second that I lost my armor, I was going to be like an ant wrestling an elephant. In the end, I was just a low-class demon, while Riser was a high-class one. Perhaps sensing my fear, Riser intensified his flames.

"Are you afraid of me?! You better be! Without your Boosted Gear, you're nothing! If you weren't hiding behind that armor of yours, you would've been dead before my fist even reached you, you hear me?! Once you take that thing off, you're useless!"

He could say whatever he wanted. So what if he was right? It was true that without the gauntlet, I was a nobody, but that wasn't going to stop me!

VII

Riser was fighting to win, no matter the cost. Fear had taken hold of my body. I wished with everything I had that I didn't have to go through this. There was no way but forward, though.

I pulled out a certain object that I'd been hiding in the back of my gauntlet.

Wham!

I slammed my fist straight into Riser's face in a cross counter. The force of the strike sent him hurling backward.

"You think that will hurt m—"

Cough!

Riser suddenly spat out a mouthful of blood before he could finish what he'd been saying. My last strike had dealt him a lethal blow.

That was only natural, of course, given what I'd had clutched in my hand.

I opened my palm to reveal it.

"A cross?! What are you doing with a cross?!" Riser cried in shock.

It wasn't just him, either. Alarmed screams rang out throughout the hall as the spectators realized what I was holding.

Yes, items like this were anathema to demons. I had been grasping the cross in my fist when I'd punched Riser.

The cross was what I'd asked Asia for before I'd gone after Rias. I'd kept it hidden until the time was right.

VI

"I boosted the power of this cross with my Sacred Gear when I hit you. An enhanced holy attack like that ought to be super-effective no matter how high-class you are. If I'm right, not even the immortal Phoenix can recover from that kind of damage."

"Are you insane?! Crosses bring nothing but raw agony to demons like us! Not even your Dragon armor should be able to protect you from—"

It was in that moment that Riser seemed to finally realize that my left arm was different now. Perhaps it hadn't been all that obvious at first sight, given the Dragon mail that encased my body. Careful inspection revealed the truth quickly enough, however.

The armor was solid and inorganic. My left arm, however, pulsated ever so slightly, as a living thing would have.

"...You gave your arm...to that thing in your gauntlet...? Is that where those lunatic powers come from...?" Riser asked, incredulous.

"I did. I offered my arm in exchange for this brief use of his strength and powers. This left arm is now the arm of a genuine Dragon. No cross will affect it."

My arm had been a necessary sacrifice for me to receive Ddraig's absolute power. It was payment so that I could stand head and shoulders above Riser in battle. My gauntlet was now part of my arm itself.

"Don't you realize you'll never be able to get it back to the way it was?!"

"So what?"

V

We could talk all day long, but the countdown was still ticking.

"If all it takes is one of my arms to bring the prez back, then that sounds like a pretty good deal to me," I said.

Riser's eyes widened in disbelief. "You're insane... So that's why you were so eager to come after me... You've gone and done it now. I'm actually impressed. Awestruck, even. Which is why..." He paused there, his fiery wings growing yet again. "I'm going to destroy you with everything I am!"

The firebird sped toward me, his whole body, and even the air around him, ablaze.

No way am I going to let you win after all this!

IV

"Hrahhhhhhhhh!"

I focused all my energy into the cross clutched in my hand! The only thing I needed was to deliver a single, overwhelming strike using that crucifix, filled with everything I had!

My fist slammed straight into Riser's oncoming punch!

Bang!

Our two ferocious powers collided. On impact, there was a brilliant flash of light that momentarily blinded me. At the same time, I could feel myself growing lighter. It was a similar sensation to when you take off your raincoat after arriving home on a rainy day.

There also came a burst of incredible heat that rushed past me. The blistering air tore through me. I had never experienced anything as dry or as intolerable before.

By the time my sight returned to me, I realized what had happened; my armor was gone!

The Scale Mail that had been protecting me had vanished! I was exposed! The only part of it that remained was my left arm, and that was only because it now belonged to the Dragon himself.

The cross had been flung from my hand from the last attack, and it lay on the floor a short distance away from me.

Hey, Dragon Emperor?! What's going on?! It hasn't been ten seconds yet! Why did my armor deactivate?! Don't tell me my arm didn't even buy me that much?!

"No, the price you paid for my power was sufficient. But you lack the essential proficiency to fully wield it. You lack training."

Are you seriously telling me that all that training with the others still wasn't enough?!

"That was but a drop in the ocean that is the life span of a demon. A demon's strength comes from decades of exercise and dedication."

I really wasn't in the mood for a lecture.

Just let me use the armor again! I pleaded. *What's the cost this time?! My eyes?! My legs?! You can have them!*

"As you are now, you can't hope to use it again in such a short span of time."

Basically, the Dragon was saying I was weak. Why was I always falling flat right when I was most needed? All I wanted was to win just this once!

"The moment the armor's energy was released, I transferred some of *my power into the jewel on your arm. It may be enough to temporarily overwhelm Riser Phenex, but that will be all. Defeating him, with his high-level regeneration ability, will require—"*

It'll require either beating him down over and over or defeating him in a single blow..., I thought back.

"Indeed. Unfortunately, what you have left will not be sufficient to pull off either of those options. Even in your boosted state, you are far from possessing enough raw power."

Yank!

Riser grabbed me by the collar, choking me as he lifted me up into the air. He flashed me a menacing grin as he wrung my neck. I couldn't breathe.

"You've done well for a Pawn. I'm impressed. I never expected you to come this far. Thanks to you, I've been able to experience the power of a Dragon firsthand. You really might've bested me with another year, even half a year, of training."

It didn't sound like Riser was joking. His gaze was deathly serious.

Another half year... In that case, hold off the engagement for six months! I thought, wishing I could've said those words.

Riser's clothes were torn, and his body was bruised and battered. Just as I had expected, recovering from an attack strengthened by a holy cross took considerable time, even for him.

His fiery wings had diminished in size, a testament to just how badly I'd hurt him.

"There's no need to feel ashamed. Once I'm married to Rias, I'll train you myself. I'll make a powerful demon out of you."

Shut up! I screamed in my mind. I definitely didn't need this guy's sympathy.

"Now then, it's time to close your eyes. I'm going to put you out for a little while. By the time you wake up, the ceremony will be over. You don't want to suffer any more than you already have, do you? I'm not a sadist, so I'll make this quick."

Riser looked sure of his victory. Had I lost? No, I would never forgive myself if I let that happen.

*   *   *

"Make sure you bring the president back with you."

I will. I made a promise, Asia.

"I will be the mightiest of Pawns!"

I will. I won't let you down, Prez!
We're going home together, Rias. Akeno, Kiba, Koneko, Asia, and I will all be there to welcome you back!

I pulled a small vial from my pocket.

"You need water to extinguish flames, right?"

What I had in my hand was a container of holy water. I had prepared it in addition to the cross before making the jump to the engagement celebration.

This kind of thing normally wouldn't have had much of an effect against a high-ranking demon. If the spectators throughout the hall had been able to see what I was holding, the most they would've done was laugh. Riser's expression, however, turned suddenly pale.

He knew about the ability I'd developed during the Rating Game, after all.

You understand exactly what's coming, don't you, Riser Phenex?

"Nooooo!"

His grip around my neck tightened. He was crushing my throat. Before he could squeeze the life from me, I pushed the stopper from the vial and hurled its contents at my opponent. Then I poured my energy into the holy water, greatly increasing its effects! Not even a high-class demon would've been able to withstand that!

"Boosted Gear Gift!"

"Transfer!"

My increased power flowed from my gauntlet into the water as it struck Riser.

"No—"

By the time Riser tried to counter what I was doing, it was too late.

The power flowing through the holy water multiplied its destructive power exponentially.

Sizzle...!

The sound of the water evaporating into steam rang throughout the hall.

Riser's wings of flame began to writhe and shrink, until he could no longer maintain their form.

The holy water seared his body, sending smoke billowing up with an awful, scorching sound.

Riser's grip on my neck weakened, and I quickly pulled myself free. Seriously, he had almost snapped my head right off!

"Gwarghhhhhhhhhh!"

Riser was thrashing around in agony from what the holy water was doing to him.

"...Is he going to die?" I wondered aloud.

"No. Even with its cleansing effects boosted, holy water won't be enough to kill a member of the Phenex clan."

Ah, all right.

"Nonetheless, the power of the holy water will consume not only his physical strength but his willpower as well. Even for a creature that regenerates from its own ashes, he will need time to recover from this blow to his spirit."

Sizzle...

The smoke and steam issuing from Riser's body gradually dissipated. When all was settled, the man was lying on the ground, wounded and weary. His clothes were in tatters.

With my new Dragon arm, I picked up the cross from where it had landed on the floor, gripped it tightly, and funneled my power into it. At the same time, I poured onto it the contents of a second vial of holy water that I had brought with me.

"Asia told me that demons are vulnerable to both the cross and holy water. So boosting the power of both at the same time ought to be pretty destructive, I'm guessing."

"Ngh…" Riser, already reeling from my last attack, made a pained face.

I glanced around to make sure there was enough room that I wasn't about to cause a problem.

"Kiba told me that I need to widen my vision and take in my opponent and their surroundings."

I focused the aura of the demonic energy flowing through me into a single point, transformed it into Dragon energy, and poured that into the cross and the holy water.

"*Transfer!*"

With this, I now had an overwhelming divine power at my disposal.

"Akeno told me that I need to gather my demonic powers inward and let the aura flow over my body. To concentrate my thoughts and to feel the wave of my energy. Even someone as useless as I am can do that."

I adjusted my stance, readying myself to deal the final blow to my opponent.

"Koneko told me to aim for the center of the body and to strike like I'm trying to carve a hole in them!"

It was my training that had taught me that. Yep, I had internalized it all. It had come in use.

With everyone's help, I was going to bring Rias back!

As I readied my attack, Riser began to panic. "H-hold on! D-don't you get it?! This engagement is for the future of all demonkind! Can't you see we need this?!"

"I don't know anything about that. But I do remember what happened when you knocked me out last time. The prez was in tears. She was crying! She was crying during this party, too! That alone is reason enough for me to come down on you hard!"

Thud!

My fist, empowered by the cross I was holding and the holy water I had poured on it, slammed straight into Riser's stomach!

"Gah!" Riser stumbled backward, coughing up blood. "I—I can't lose… Not like this…" With those final words, he fell flat to the ground, unable to get back up.

I glanced down at Riser's motionless body before approaching Rias.

A figure leaped between us. It was Riser's sister, Ravel. She glared at me in silence, as if wanting to issue some kind of complaint.

I, however, pointed at her with my Dragon arm and said: "If you have something to say, go ahead and spit it out. I'll take you on anytime!"

Perhaps because of the gravity of my challenge, she backed away.

I walked right past her without so much as a second glance, then stood before Rias. "Let's go home, Prez," I said with a warm smile.

"...Issei..."

Next, I turned my eyes to the person standing beside her, Rias's father.

He had the same crimson hair as his daughter, and he sported an aristocratic, dandy-like appearance.

As I faced him, I gave a deep bow. "The prez, my master Rias Gremory, is coming with me. Please forgive my impudence, but I will be taking her home now," I declared.

Rias's father said nothing in reply. Instead, he merely closed his eyes in quiet resignation. Sirzechs had been seated on Rias's opposite side earlier but was now nowhere to be found.

I would've liked to thank him, but that was going to have to wait until the next time I met him.

Taking Rias's hand, I pulled the piece of paper that Grayfia had given me from my pocket. She'd instructed me to use the magic circle on the reverse side once I'd reached Rias.

As promised, when I turned the card over, another magic circle was already letting off a brilliant glow.

Suddenly, a giant winged, four-legged creature leaped out of it. It looked to be something like a cross between an eagle and a lion.

"A griffin...," I heard someone murmur in the background.

Does Grayfia want me to escape with the prez on the back of this weird thing?

I climbed onto its back and took Rias's hand to help her up behind me.

Rwhhhhh!

The griffin let out a powerful roar before beginning to flap its great wings back and forth as it took off for the gaping crater that I had earlier smashed through the wall.

"We'll see you all back in the clubroom!" I cried out to the others, who waved in return with smiles on their faces.

Atop the griffin, Rias and I soared deep into the underworld.

Father×Father

"Lord Phenex, I'm very sorry that the engagement between my daughter and your son ended in this way. I know it's rude of me to ask this, but would you perhaps—?"

"Say no more, Lord Gremory. This would have been a good marriage between two fine pure-blooded demons, but it would appear that all parties concerned may have been acting out of more than a touch of avarice. We both already have pure-blooded grandchildren to our names. Perhaps, being demons, we cannot help but desire the absolute best? Or perhaps we pushed this so hard because of the hell we witnessed during the last war?"

"…No, I would say that I merely forced my own desires on my daughter."

"Hyoudou. That was his name, am I correct? I would like to thank him. What my son lacked most was knowledge of defeat. He placed too much faith in our clan's unique abilities. What happened today will serve as a valuable lesson for him. The Phoenix is not invincible. If this engagement has done nothing more than teach him that, then I am grateful, Lord Gremory."

"Lord Phenex…"

"Your daughter has a fine servant in her charge. I suspect the underworld will not be lacking for excitement in the months to come."

"…Yet I would never have expected my daughter to acquire something so terrible."

"The Welsh Dragon. I wouldn't have believed that such a fearsome thing truly existed, had I not witnessed it with my own eyes."

"Then it won't be long until..."

"Indeed. In fact, it may already be out there somewhere."

"The Vanishing Dragon... It will only be a matter of time before Red meets White..."

Last Kiss

Unlike in the human world, the sky in the demon realm was a rich purple in color.

It gave me an uncanny feeling, yet it somehow managed to put me at ease. Perhaps that was because I was a demon.

As I stared up at that strange sky, Rias's hand brushed against my cheek.

"Silly Issei," she said with an embarrassed smile. Judging from her expression, she appeared relieved to have finally escaped from her painful predicament.

"—!" That look changed, however, when her gaze fell upon my left arm. Her eyes sorrowful, she touched it lightly with her fingers.

I suppose that made sense. My left arm was covered now in red scales, and it sported razor-sharp talons and an overall rough, bestial appearance.

"Your arm... You gave it to the Dragon in exchange for that power, didn't you?"

"Yeah, but it was worth it. What's one arm from a useless guy like me compared to that ultimate power? Thanks to that deal, I managed to take down Riser and bring you home!" I replied with a forced smile.

Rias's eyes, however, glistened with sadness. "It won't go back to the way it was, you know."

"Ah, that could cause a few problems. I guess I can tell people it's a cosplay item? It might raise a few eyebrows at school, though... Huh? What's wrong?"

"Asia will cry when she finds out."

...*Ugh, she's right. Why am I always bringing Asia to tears?*

"...And you do understand that while you may have broken off my engagement this time, it won't be the last we hear of it, right? If you keep this up..." Rias trailed off there, her voice steeped in sorrow.

I pushed myself to laugh. "Then I'll give my right arm next time. And my eyes the time after that. I'll do whatever it takes to protect you. Nothing will stop me. I'm your Pawn, after all. It's my job, right?"

—*!*

At that moment, something pressed against my mouth.

Rias had put her hands around my neck and was pressing her lips to mine.

A kiss.

It wasn't a particularly deep one, and while it didn't involve either of our tongues, I could sense the depth of Rias's emotions through those soft, delicate lips of hers. The rich suppleness of her skin and the beautiful aroma of her crimson hair brought my thoughts to a standstill.

After remaining that way for close to a minute, Rias pulled back and let out a soft chuckle.

It was right about then that my brain started working again.

......

A k-kiss?! R-Rias just kissed me! And I kissed her!

It felt like my head was going to explode!

"That was my first kiss. In Japan, that's considered quite a monumental moment, isn't it?" Rias asked.

"A-ah, right! Hold on, your first kiss?!"

I was taken aback by the confession. I mean, a first kiss was supposed to be incredibly important for a young woman, right?!

"R-r-really?! W-with me?!"

"What you did was certainly worth a kiss, wouldn't you say? Think of it as your reward," Rias replied with a bright smile.

What is even happening right now?! I thought in disbelief. Everything I'd gone through had all been worth it just for that kiss alone!

"Speaking of firsts, do you really want my virginity that much?"

"I do!" I responded at once before catching myself. Perhaps I'd been just a touch too honest.

It was the truth, though. There was no doubt that I wanted it! So much so that I'd been willing to blurt it out in front of all those people back there!

"...You really are up-front about lewd things, aren't you?" Rias looked a little troubled by my admission, but she was still smiling.

Truthfully, I kind of wanted to apologize for being so obsessed with that kind of thing. As I mentally reprimanded myself, Rias began to pat my cheek, laughing happily.

Thank goodness, I thought. It came as no small relief to see her smiling like her old self again.

New Life

"And that is why I, Rias Gremory, will be moving in with you. Thank you for your guidance and encouragement, Father, Mother."

We were in the living room of the Hyoudou residence, my house. The crimson-haired beauty sitting beside me was greeting my parents, while the blond-haired beauty at my other side looked ready to break down into tears.

Asia didn't appear to be taking this development all that well.

After everything that'd happened in the demon realm, Rias had suddenly announced that she would be coming to live with me.

At the time, I hadn't realized exactly what Rias meant, but she'd been quite insistent. *"I want to deepen my relationship with my dear servant,"* she'd said. I had to wonder if my house was really the best place for that.

Perhaps I just had no affinity for comprehending how high-class demons thought.

Thus, the engagement between the Houses of Gremory and Phenex had been called off. The prez seemed happy about it, and really, that's all I'd wanted.

Supposedly, Riser had taken his first-ever defeat pretty hard. He'd even withdrawn from the public eye.

"Oh my. First Asia, now Rias. It's like we have two daughters now."

My mom had taken a liking to Asia ever since she'd moved in with us, so she looked overjoyed at the prospect of having another young woman in the house. Likewise, my father was crying tears of joy.

"Yep, yep. This is like a dream come true. A household of girls! I would have killed for this back when I was a kid!"

Now it all makes sense. I suppose I was my father's son in that way. We even shared the same sort of dreams.

As for the problem of my left arm...

While technically still the limb of a Dragon, Rias's and Akeno's efforts had forced it to return to the appearance of a human arm so that it wouldn't interfere with my day-to-day.

From what I gathered, it wouldn't return to its Dragon form so long as we prevented the accumulation of Dragon magic inside it. However, the act of dispelling that buildup had to be performed every few days.

Sure, it was a bit troublesome, but I'd been able to get the prez back. Compared to that, the price felt relatively cheap.

Plus, the way that Rias and Akeno had dispelled the magic was incredibly erotic. Heh, I would never have expected them to do that kind of thing for me... I started thinking that maybe this new arm was a good thing after all.

Ddraig had gone quiet after my fight with Riser. Even when I called out to him, he didn't answer. There were still a lot of questions I wanted answered.

Just who was that White One he kept mentioning? It sounded like whoever it was, they were going to show up eventually. I suspected I'd have to deal with that before long.

"Well, Issei. Now that I've received your parents' permission, I'll be living here from now on. I wonder whether you might carry my belongings up to my room?" Rias instructed with a flick of her crimson hair.

"O-okay!"

"I'll help, Issei," Asia said, following after me. Under her breath, she muttered, "...Ah, maybe the best I can hope for is polygyny... But... But... That's a violation of the Lord's teachings... But at this rate... Ngh..."

"Huh? What does *'polygyny'* mean?" I asked.

"Nothing!" Asia replied quickly, averting her gaze.

She's been in a bad mood ever since Rias arrived. Do they not get along?

"Now, Issei. Put that over there," the prez instructed me the moment we reached her room.

"Okay!"

"Issei, let's take a bath once you're finished... I'll wash your back for you."

"Seriously?!"

That's fine with me! You can do it every day if you like!

"Ah! If you're going to bathe together, then let me join you! Don't leave me out!" Asia begged.

No, Asia, stop! I wanted to cry out. *If you start fighting over me, I won't be able to keep myself under control!*

"I'm sorry, Asia, but that's how it is. Could this perhaps be a declaration of war on your part?" Rias inquired.

"I don't want to lose. Why do things never go my way?" replied Asia.

I could almost see the sparks flying between the two of them.

Whether Rias or Asia, I just couldn't understand what went on in the minds of women!

Will a harem even be possible at this rate? I wondered. There was one thing I knew for certain, however...

My everyday life was about to get much more interesting.

AFTERWORD

How many times have I used the word *breasts* in the first and second volumes of *High School DxD*?

Write the correct answer on a postcard and send it my way for the chance to win one of twenty mouse pads shaped after Rias's very own chest! Ha, just kidding. I'm not offering any prizes like that.

Ishibumi here. It's good to see you again. What did you think of Volume 2?

The series is really starting to turn pornographic, huh? At this rate, not even I, the author, can fully picture how the next volume will turn out. Incidentally, you may be wondering what that erotic way of dispelling the Dragon power in Issei's arm was. You'll have to wait until the next volume to find out!

And thanks to Rias's negative influence, you can look forward to Asia becoming a natural at pure eroticism, too.

Yep, it's going to be a volume that middle school students and high school students alike will be embarrassed to purchase in stores!

I'm a bit worried that someone might impose an age limit on it, but this is a light novel series in the style of a *shōnen* manga, after all, so please bear with me!

Just like the Boosted Gear's Gift technique, all Sacred Gears possess insane power-ups called Balance Breakers that they can activate when they're pushed way past their limits.

Asia and Kiba will certainly be able to activate those techniques when driven to extremes, too. Think of it like Super Saiyans in *Dragon Ball* or a Bankai in *Bleach*.

Issei ignored the usual requirements for activating a Balance Breaker when drawing on the Red Dragon Emperor's power, and then he went on to use it excessively, so he had to offer his arm in sacrifice to rectify the situation. On top of that, given how inexperienced he was, he couldn't unleash that power at its full potential.

I've called these techniques Balance Breakers because they destroy the equilibrium that holds the world together.

But with these new abilities, Issei is now no longer just a fighter; he can also work to support his friends and allies.

I wonder when we will meet the new rival character, this White Dragon?

Now then, on to my thanks.

To my editor H, for leading me down the path of becoming a pornographic author: Thanks for always looking out for me. I hope you enjoy yourself each time I strip one of the characters naked.

To Miyama-Zero, for all the beautiful and mesmerizing illustrations: Do accept my apologies for being so fussy about the development of the designs. I look forward to seeing the next set of images!

With that, please look forward to Volume 3. I hope you're anticipating seeing Rias's breasts again as much as I am.